SOULS ON FIRE

MEMOIRS OF A TWIN FLAME TRUE LOVE JOURNEY

MICHELLE WHITE | JUSTIN WHITE

DIVINE LOVE ENTERPRISES LLC

Cover design by Silvana G. Sánchez © SP Designs
www.selfpubdesigns.com

❀ Created with Vellum

This story is dedicated to you.

May you find what you're looking for.

PART I

Upon meeting, you hand every member of your Soul
Family a costume and a script.

—

CHAPTER 1

June 2015

*W*alking toward the crowded Red Robin at lunchtime, I prepared for an awkward get-to-know-you conversation. Portland's early summer sunshine lit up the cheerful pink blouse floating over my body. That blouse was a liar. It didn't reflect the me underneath. Inside I was colorless, hopeless, empty. I wore that blouse because I had no idea what my favorite color was. As was my custom with every man I met online, I asked your favorite color during our early conversation. Then I wore that color when we met. Yours is the only answer I remember from a field of dozens of men. Maybe a hundred men. Your favorite color, you said, was pink. I thought, *"This guy won't work out. I don't like pink."*

Despite the difference of opinion, I agreed to meet you over lunch. How could I not? Your avatar commanded my attention from the first moment it turned up in my Ashley Madison search. Though only an image of the bright blue iris and deep black pupil of your eye, it was a siren song for me.

Crossing into the restaurant, a shiver that had nothing to do with the air temperature gripped me. It was the kind of chill my grandpa used to say meant a goose walked over my grave. Inside my head, I heard a whisper.

"He's sitting under the light."

My eyes roved to the back wall of the restaurant, slightly to the left of the main walkway. An unnatural light shone down from the high ceiling. It was a golden cone, extending earthward from a point somewhere out of sight but not far above the roof. I felt the pull of you waiting there like a physical sensation, a hook in my chest straight through my sternum to my shoulder blades. The hostess noticed me.

"Party of one?" she chirped.

"No, I'm meeting someone."

"Do you want to look around for them?" she asked as I passed by.

"I already know where he is."

I felt your eyes on my face when I turned toward the booth where you waited. I smiled, thinking how good-looking you were in person and feeling the deep thrill of immediate attraction. You stood as I closed the distance between us. My eyes were caught by yours, magnetized. They were the same blue I'd seen on your profile, but I was sure I knew them from somewhere else. As my body edged into the imaginary cone of light, time did something weird, ticking simultaneously

4

slower and faster. We shook hands. Dust motes danced in the light, and the voice whispered again.

"There's no light fixture. Those are stars."

Time snapped back to normal speed. We sat across from each other and embarked on a familiar conversation, spoken by millions of would-be cheating spouses, over millions of collective years, in millions of lifetimes.

"What are you looking for?" you asked. I stuck to the partially true story I told all the men I hooked up with.

"I have a good marriage, but I need someone who can keep up with me in bed. I met my husband when I was 21, during our junior year of college. We got married when we were 24. Everything was good for a long time, but as we got older, our sex drives went way out of sync."

"That's pretty much the same with me. Have you found anyone yet?"

"I've been having an affair for a couple of months. It's worked out well, but he's moving to Canada with his wife and kids next month. I'm looking for someone to replace him. How about you, what's your story?"

"I've met up with a lot of ladies over the years. A couple turned into long-term affairs, but I got caught by my wife about a year ago. That's my biggest concern," your voice grew fervent. "She cannot find out about another affair! Finding out about the other one hurt her so much. She doesn't deserve that pain."

"I'm in the same boat," I assured you. "My husband found out about my first affair. It was awful. This sounds silly, but I love him and I don't want to hurt him again. Plus, I have two little kids to protect."

"I understand," it was your turn to reassure me. "We don't have kids of our own, but we're foster parents for my wife's nephew." The server materialized. You ordered a Chicken Ensenada Platter and a Diet Coke. I ordered the Avo-Cobb-O Salad and iced tea with lemon. As she bustled off, our gazes locked for a fraction of a second. The intensity was unbearable. Our eyes skittered in opposite directions, and I cleared my throat to speak.

"So, am I the first woman you've met up with since your wife found out?"

"No, there have been a few, but no one has clicked. I'm being extra careful. There are a lot of ladies out there looking for a man to get them out of their marriage. That won't be me; I will never divorce my wife."

"Same here! Divorce is absolutely out of the question."

"Good," you sighed, relieved. "I need someone stable and independent because sometimes I'm out of touch for days at a time. There can't be any emotional attachment between us."

"We are totally on the same page," I said. "I hate clingy behavior, and I'm not interested in chat." Usually, I was the one introducing all the rules at these interviews.

"There's one more thing," you continued down your checklist.

"What's that?"

"There may be a day when I just disappear. If anything threatens my marriage, if my wife even tells me she's suspicious, whether it's about you or not, I'll cut you off. I've done it before."

"I get it!" This was like talking to myself in a mirror. "It wouldn't be personal, just self-preservation. What we're doing isn't about love. It's about getting our physical needs met."

"Exactly!" you exclaimed. The intensity between us steadied to a warm thrum. Our meal arrived, and we ate together for the first time.

"Where are you from?" I asked.

"I was born and raised just up the road in Oregon City. Are you from here?"

"No, we moved here last September from San Francisco. We got tired of the rat race, plus the kids suffered because of our careers, so we decided I'd stop working and stay home for a few years. We chose Portland because it's cheaper and close to my husband's family."

"Where did you work?" you asked.

"I was a vice president at a big company in San Francisco."

"A vice president?" You sounded far more impressed than you needed to be.

"Yeah, it wasn't a big deal. I was in finance, working with Wall Street. Really boring stuff." I did not want to dwell on my nightmarish career. "What do you do?"

"I manage a discount tool store in Vancouver." Your answer disappointed me.

"So, you live *and* work over there?" We were talking

a 30-mile drive to see each other, which would be hellish in Portland's traffic. You foresaw my objection.

"It's a long drive, but we wouldn't be able to see each other often, so maybe we can try it out?" I pretended momentary reluctance. In truth, I had other options waiting in the wings. Willing men lived closer to me, and I could unearth a dozen more co-conspirators with ease, but I'd long lost the ability to say no or stand up for what I wanted. You smiled, capturing me again in your blue stare; I knew your eyes despite not recognizing you. The golden cone fluxed briefly.

"All right, we'll see how it goes," I agreed.

"So, you said you have two kids, right? How old are they?"

"My son is ten, and my daughter is seven. How old is your nephew?"

"My wife's nephew," you were quick to clarify. "He's fifteen. He's lived with us since he was eight." I could feel that you were uncomfortable with this subject, so I changed it.

"When did you figure out you were looking for something more than you had with your wife?" I liked how you paused and thought a moment before answering.

"At first when I cheated, I did it to find out if sex felt different with someone other than my wife. See, I was overweight all my life. In my late 20's, I was so sick I had to go into urgent care — back then, I avoided regular appointments as much as possible — and the doctor told me I would be lucky if I lived past 40. I had high blood pressure and kidney damage. It took me another ten years, but I finally decided I didn't want to die like that. I wanted to be in control of my body and my life. Once I made it about what I wanted for myself, I was able to lose the weight and keep it off. My highest was 350 pounds, and I worked my way down to 165."

"Whoa," it was my turn to be impressed; I hadn't seen the other side of 200 since I was in college. "How'd you do it?"

"I eliminated so much from my diet, like carbs and soda. I filled up on veggies and water. I found exercises I enjoyed doing and started doing them as much as I could. Once I lost some weight, my confidence went up, and it got easier to lose more. Women started to pay attention to me, and I realized I was attractive. When that happened, I started to question why I was unhappy besides my weight, and that led to the affairs."

"I've struggled with my weight since childhood," I shared. "I hate being overweight, but no amount of dieting or exercise ever worked."

"I'm attracted to women of all shapes and sizes," you gave me a pointed once-over. "I think you're very attractive, and I like your self-confidence."

"Thanks, same to you!" I batted my eyelashes to make you laugh.

The conversation carried us for another hour before we split the bill. Walking side-by-side toward the parking lot, we paused at the same moment to face each other. My heart sped up. Instead of kissing me goodbye, as I expected, you asked a question.

"Do you want to go somewhere and kiss?" Another

thrill shot through me. This was not the same pattern as other first meetings I'd experienced.

"Yes, I'd like that," I said as desire pierced me in the same spot where I felt the hook at the outset of our date. "Shall we take my car?"

"Sure." You followed me. Climbing in the driver's seat, I cast about for an idea of where to go.

"IKEA parking lot?" I suggested. You nodded.

The sky clouded over and rain began to fall. We parked in the new grayness of the day, while IKEA blue and yellow loomed through the car windows. Raindrops pattered on the sunroof as electricity built between us, and around us, in the interior of the car. We leaned toward each other. Our lips met. Lightning struck, and I couldn't breathe. I felt my chest come apart where the hook had set before. The Earth I lived on came unglued at the equator, each hemisphere twisting violently in opposition to the other, before clunking back together with a deep finality. Our bodies jerked back from each other. There was no difficulty in holding our gazes locked at that moment.

"What was that?" you demanded, breathless.

"I don't know. You felt it, too?" I couldn't wait to feel your lips on mine again.

"Yes! I've never felt anything like that before."

We leaned in simultaneously to continue kissing. The electricity invaded our bodies, and we breathed the spark between us into flame as our kisses grew. I never wanted that feeling to end.

CHAPTER 2

Two years earlier…

"Something's wrong with my arm," I announced in a high-pitched voice that carried the edge of an argument. "It's been bugging me for miles."

We were paused in stop-and-go traffic, simmering in Los Angeles summer smog. The Getty Museum perched on a cliff over my left shoulder. My husband rode in the passenger's seat while the kids stared at a Disney movie delivered via the entertainment system.

"It's probably asleep," Ed offered. "You've been driving a long time with it in one position." My arm was pins and needles. My heart thundered, and a muscle twinged under my jawline.

"Look up the symptoms of a heart attack," I instructed.

"You're not having a heart attack."

"Look them up!" He pulled out his phone and read aloud.

"The most common symptom of a heart attack is chest pain or discomfort. Pain may travel into the shoulder, arm, back, neck, or jaw."

"And?"

"The discomfort may feel like heartburn. Symptoms may include shortness of breath, nausea, feeling faint, a cold sweat, or feeling tired."

"I told you, I've been lightheaded and tired for the past few days. Now my left arm hurts. What if I'm having a heart attack?" Before he could reply, Elsie's five-year-old bladder struck.

"Mommy? I need to go potty." We'd stopped not a half-hour earlier for the same reason.

"Elsie, do you really have to go?"

"Yes, Mommy."

"Great! Now we have to find a bathroom," I grumbled. Ed was already searching.

"There's a Costco close by," he said, directing me through side streets to the crowded parking lot.

"I'm scared," I admitted as I put the car in park. "I don't feel right."

"Let's get home. You can see the doctor tomorrow if you still feel unwell. Nothing's going to happen to you between now and then."

While I waited for Elsie in the bathroom, I googled the closest hospital and debated taking the time for an ER visit. We'd overstayed our vacation in San Diego, and neither Ed nor I could afford another day away from work. The pain under my jaw throbbed in sync with the pain in my arm. More than anything, I wanted someone to validate how I felt.

As I navigated out of the parking lot, my thoughts picked up speed. What if I was genuinely sick? What if I passed out and crashed the car? On the freeway, the what-if game continued. My head began to ache as my worry ping-ponged from heart attack to stroke. We crawled along in traffic. The more I dwelled on the pains, the more pronounced they became. Unable to contain my fear any longer, I attacked Ed.

"Why don't you want me to go to the hospital?"

"Do you think you need to go to a hospital?" he sounded confused.

"I'm going to the hospital NOW!" My shout startled Eddie, who'd been watching the movie while all this happened.

"Mommy? What's wrong?" In the rearview mirror, his big green eyes, so like mine, were worried.

"Shell, if you need to go to the hospital, then we'll go," Ed smoothed things over. "How do we find a hospital that takes our insurance down here?" His helplessness galled me, but I'd won.

"I already looked one up. It's back by Costco."

"Why didn't you say so before we got on the freeway again?" I pressed my lips together and changed lanes to exit.

AFTER DEPOSITING Ed and the kids in the packed waiting room, I stood in line at check-in, cradling my left arm.

The admissions nurse prompted me across a white laminate desk.

"First name?" She plodded through endless questions about identity and insurance. "Why are you seeking emergency care?" I began describing my symptoms in minute detail.

"...and that's why I think I'm having a heart attack. It makes sense! I'm stressed all the time. I'm overweight, and I never exercise. Plus, I haven't been eating well lately." The nurse's eyes were glazed over.

"Is that all?" she asked. Red-faced, I nodded. "The ER is experiencing high patient volume. Please return to the waiting area. You'll be called when there's a bed available. If your symptoms worsen—"

"I said, I think I'm having a heart attack. Isn't that an emergency?"

"Mrs., uh..." she squinted at her screen, "Black, you'd be a lot more distressed if you were having a heart attack. But now you're here, and you'll be safe if you *do* have a heart attack. Please go to the waiting area. We'll call you when a bed is available." She turned to the next person in line. Ed looked up when I approached.

"How long's the wait?"

"She didn't give an estimate!" I snapped. We alternated bathroom visits with the kids and suffered the hope/disappointment cycle each time the swinging doors opened to reveal a nurse's head poking out to call someone else's name. By the two-hour mark, my symptoms had vanished. I turned to Ed reluctantly. "I feel better. This is a waste of time."

"What do you want to do?" he asked.

"I want to leave, but what if we get out in the middle of nowhere and I have a heart attack?" I rushed past my doubt before he could respond to it and added, "Yeah, I guess I want to leave."

"Okay, let's go then." He roused the kids, and they debated what fast food joint to hit for dinner as we walked toward the parking garage. I couldn't shake the feeling that something terrible was going to happen to me. Breathing became difficult as disastrous scenarios filled me with dread. My arm started to tingle.

"I feel wrong again," I said. Ed looked at me. The surprise on his face confirmed my fears.

"Oh! You're very pale."

"Get dinner for the kids," I spun around. "I'm going back."

Ed and the kids had not yet returned to the waiting room when I heard my name called. I followed the nurse through a maze of hallways and changed into the gown she handed me. Behind a flimsy blue curtain, I settled on the bed, where I shut my eyes and tried to ignore the tingling.

A couple of hours later, an EKG cart pushed into my space. While the technician worked, I asked if it looked like I was having a heart attack.

"The doctor will be in to give you the results," was all he said. Another hour passed. A blood draw cart arrived and departed. Late in the evening, the curtain drew back to reveal a young man wearing a stethoscope. He shook my hand.

"Mrs. Black, what brings you to the ER?" I recited a litany of every pain, and every speculation, that had run through my brain. The doctor nodded, making notes. When I concluded, he smiled.

"First, let me assure you, you're not having a heart attack. Your EKG and blood tests look good. There's nothing wrong with your heart at all. In fact, it appears very healthy." My mouth fell open.

"Well, I didn't imagine the things I felt!"

"I know you didn't. You told me your life is stressful. You don't have time to take care of yourself between work, kids, and your marriage. Since I don't see much physically wrong with you, this leads me to believe you suffered a panic attack. I'm prescribing Xanax to treat your anxiety. See your regular doctor in a week to follow up."

It took a minute to digest his words. I knew what Xanax was from the movies. Specifically, from Anne Heche's character in *Six Days, Seven Nights*. Enduring the stress of a plane crash on a remote island, she downed one after another of them before collapsing into a drugged stupor. Each time she took one, she parroted her doctor's orders, *'They're for situations of high tension!'* Ed and I often quoted the line to each other. The diagnosis felt like an accusation.

"I don't have panic attacks! I'm calm! Capable! I was a straight-A student through college, and I'm a vice president at a *huge* corporation in San Francisco!" I ticked off reasons on my fingers. "I don't freak out about anything. I'm in complete control of my life. Something must be wrong with me. How do you test for a stroke?"

"Experiencing stress is not a weakness, you know," he explained patiently. "Most people have trouble coping from time to time. You need to find ways to relax, so you don't *give* yourself a heart attack. The in-hospital pharmacy will fill your prescription, and the nurse will bring it to you. After that, you're free to go," he signed the paper with a flourish, then looked up to see tears in my eyes. "You're going to be okay. Do you have anyone to talk to? You should think about getting a therapist. It's amazing how talking through your worries can help alleviate them."

When he was gone, I unwound the hospital gown from around my waist and slipped back into my street clothes. A nurse appeared with a little orange pill bottle containing thirty Xanax tablets. She shooed me out. I emerged from the swinging doors to find my family in the still-packed waiting area. Elsie hugged my knees while Eddie remained absorbed in his tablet.

"No heart attack?" Ed asked.

"No, my heart is good," I paused. "But, I have a prescription for Xanax."

"Are you serious?" Despite his attempt to keep the amusement out of his voice, I was defensive.

"I had a panic attack! The doctor told me they cause physical symptoms."

"Okay. Do you want me to drive first?"

"No."

"Are you sure?"

"I said, no! I'll drive first." I hoped driving would erase the doctor's words, and Ed's laughter, echoing in my head.

A COUPLE OF HOURS LATER, we stopped at a hotel in the middle of nowhere. After we tucked in the sleeping kids, I was ready to talk about the ER visit.

"I'm sorry about today," I began.

"It's okay, Shell," Ed rushed to reassure me. "I'm glad you got a clean bill of health. Now we know your heart is good for decades more!"

"I don't exactly have a clean bill of health. There's the panic attack."

"You already said you're tired, plus you're stressed about getting home on time. It isn't like this will happen again."

I wanted to say, *"But what if it does?"* Instead, I said, "Yeah, I'm sure you're right." Anxiety rose in my chest. I had a name for it now.

"Did you take one of your pills?" Ed asked in the dark.

"Yes." I couldn't tell if the feeling of being swallowed up by the bed was a real physical sensation or one caused by the medicine entering my bloodstream. "I don't need them. I shouldn't have taken one."

"Worst case is you'll sleep really well!" He was right, but not for the reason he thought. I'd taken a Xanax, but I'd also taken two OxyContin that I fished from the depths of my baggage in the trunk. Teasingly, he added, "And now you'll always be prepared for those 'high tension situations!'"

I couldn't bring myself to laugh. The air conditioner chugged, and the sinking-into-the-mattress sensation became more pronounced. Ed snored. I listened to it a while before I followed him into sleep.

CHAPTER 3

*B*ack in Silicon Valley, life returned to its hectic baseline. While Ed worked from home, I commuted to downtown San Francisco. Eddie and Elsie spent their weeks at summer camps with enticing names like *Sports Jam* and *Mad Science!* Weekends brought baseball games and backyard parties, replete with racks of ribs and tequila shots raised in toasts with other parents who were our friends.

Independence Day that year fell on a Thursday. Wednesday, I sat at my fifteenth-floor desk, half-hearing the distant cable car bells that pierced the morning fog. Unable to focus on the mountain of work piling up, I lapsed into mentally reciting my to-do list for the hundredth time. I reached for a pen. I wrote the list and crumpled it up, tossing it to join a dozen siblings in my wastepaper basket. I started anew on a fresh piece of paper. The ringing phone broke my trance.

"I'm glad you called," I said to Ed. "I'm going over

the errands we have to do before tomorrow." My mom, stepdad, and aunt were arriving for a visit the next day, and we were hosting a holiday pool party at our house.

"I can't go with you on the road trip to Eddie's tournament next week," Ed dropped his news. "I have to be on-call for a customer in Oakland." I let the silence speak my disapproval. "And...someone scheduled a conference call this afternoon that goes till six o'clock. Can you cover the party errands without me?"

"Fine, I have to go! Bye," I mashed down the do not disturb button and silenced my cell before leaning back. The arrival of my boss, Monica, shook me from a daydream.

"Good morning, Michelle!"

"Good morning," I yawned. Monica paused, her key poised in midair.

"Is everything okay?" she asked. I couldn't stop myself from complaining.

"I'm totally exhausted. I barely slept last night after responding to endless emails from Jay," I invoked our CFO's name, and a fictitious email exchange. "To tell the truth, I haven't felt right since my ER visit. I keep having dizzy spells, and now I'm short of breath." I felt Monica's reaction, a mixture of sympathy and frustration tempered by her tiredness. I hated that I could feel what my coworkers felt when they interacted with me. I could feel what everyone around me was feeling. Growing up, my dad tried to squash the empathic sense out of me. He insisted, "It's impossible to know what another person is feeling." Or, "You're imagining things, so stop pretending to do something you can't." When I displayed emotions that mismatched my surroundings, he'd squat on my level and threaten, "You're overly-sensitive! Get ahold of yourself!" I was never sensitive on purpose. It was merely who I was; an ultra-fine-tuned antenna, picking up every emotional current around me. I tried to ignore my empathy because he told me to, but that was like trying to ignore my two fully functional eyes. Monica finally responded.

"I'm sorry to hear that! I hope you start feeling better soon," she slid into her office and shut the door fast. I doodled on my aborted to-do list, hoping for a return of the elusive symptoms of a panic attack. Fifteen minutes later, my phone rang.

"Can you please come to the conference room? Bring the new intern." I decoded the undertone of stress in Monica's voice. Another acquisition was launching. In confirmation, I overheard my coworker, Josh, exclaim.

"Here we go again!" Josh enjoyed the distinction of being chosen for the elite acquisition team. I resented it. I collected our intern, shiny-faced and dressed to the nines in a size zero designer skirt suit that matched her lip color. Looking down as we approached the conference room, I contemplated my tired sweater set and elastic waistband pants, bought at a plus-size outlet store. Pins and needles prickled inside my left shoulder as I lowered into my chair. My heart raced, then it beat an extra time. I'd never felt that before. Monica called the meeting to order.

"This is a quick turnaround, folks. Faster than ever."

Her words evoked a three-month-old memory and I lost track of the meeting.

MY PHONE VIBRATED me out of a dream.

"Hello?" I rasped. From my hotel bed in Denver, a thousand miles away, I felt Monica's relief before she spoke.

"I'm so glad you picked up! We've got a fast turnaround on an acquisition opportunity. I need you on the kickoff call this afternoon." This vacation was the first respite I'd had in the three months since I returned to work, weeks ahead of schedule, from medical leave. I tried to be firm.

"I can work this morning, but I have wedding events this afternoon." Before Monica could reply, my resolve crumbled. "I guess I can work tomorrow morning, too."

"Oh, thank you!" She launched into a list of what she needed while I silently berated myself for my weakness. Ed eyed me from under half-closed lids after I said goodbye.

"What's up with Monica?"

"There's another rush acquisition! I have to present my analysis Sunday afternoon." His lack of reaction irked me. "That means I have to work today and tomorrow!"

"Did you tell her no?" This was the opening gauntlet in an argument we'd been jousting at for months.

"You know there's no one else to do the work!"

"That's because you didn't force her to hire backup before your surgery."

"Like it's *my* fault they started an acquisition binge a week into my recovery," I declaimed. A small voice piped up.

"Good morning, Momma!" We'd woken Elsie. It irritated me that my daughter was witnessing this argument.

"Elsie, go back to sleep!" I snapped. Hurt flashed in her little brown eyes as she struggled to understand my reaction.

"She won't go back to sleep," Ed clucked at me. "It's after eight o'clock!" I checked my impatience but failed to apologize. Elsie grilled him about our plan for the day while I woke Eddie, who stretched and started talking. His cheerful stream-of-consciousness flowed as he trotted after me through the hotel suite.

"Mom, I dreamed about the wedding. I'm going to dance all night!" He'd chattered for weeks about the reception. "Mom, look, here's my newest combat move - look!" I had to watch him roundhouse-and-slash, or he'd never stop insisting. "Mom, I'm hungry. I want hot dogs. When's breakfast?" I couldn't take it anymore.

"Eddie, be quiet!" I felt my words crush him, yet, again, failed to apologize. My temper shortened as the morning progressed. In the hotel restaurant, I was rude to the server and snapped at my mom. After breakfast, we met up with other wedding guests in the lobby. I growled that I had to work and limped off. Ed caught me a minute later.

"Where are the kids?" I asked, suspicious.

"With Grams and Pop."

"What are you doing?"

"I'm going to check work email." He caught the look that brewed in my eyes. "Don't worry! I promised Grams I'd help with the kids after." Pacified, I leaned on my crutches and unleashed my upset feelings.

"I'm so pissed at Monica. She knows I'm at a wedding! She shouldn't have asked me to work. This whole trip is ruined! I'm going to insist we hire a full-time analyst. Jay is going to have to approve it or risk losing me."

"It's about time!" Ed crowed. I slipped into the bathroom to swallow a Vicodin for my tender knee and got to work as the medicine's veil descended.

Two hours later, I paused between spreadsheets and slides. Ed was still in the room.

"I thought you were going to help my mom and Matt with the kids?"

"Something came up at work," he answered without looking at me. Pretending to pass by to use the bathroom, I snuck a peek at his screen. He was reading one of his favorite tech websites, and his phone displayed hockey scores.

"You're not working!" I exploded. "Why did you lie to me? How could you abandon my mom like that?" Much to my surprise, Ed responded with equal anger.

"You're acting like a brat! Stop taking your work frustrations out on everyone. It's your fault you're in this situation. You could've said no, but you didn't. Don't make us pay for your bad decisions!"

"What do you want me to do?" I narrowed my eyes. "Quit? Refuse to do my work and get fired? How are we supposed to pay the bills if that happens? We're still digging out from the last time *you* got a new job!" My empath sense absorbed the feeling of his ego bruising.

"You know I couldn't help getting laid off," he muttered. It was true he'd been laid off from his most recent position, but I was talking about older hurts. I pressed my lips together and chose the path of avoidance.

"I need to call Monica now, and I have a call tomorrow morning. After that, I should be done until Sunday." Ed's pinched look eased.

"All right, we can make this work." The argument was over, a landmine buried in the breach between us. "I'll head to the pool. Text me when you're done."

When the door shut behind him, I ran for my Vicodin and shook one out. I wavered, then dropped it back in the bottle. My knee didn't hurt anymore.

A minute later, I dialed Monica. She picked up before the first ring finished.

"Michelle? I'm glad you called! All the assumptions are changing — I'll put you on speaker. Josh is here." We spent the next hour rehashing my morning tasks. I wanted to scream, throw the phone, hang up on them. In the end, I faced two hours of work to redo. Monica apologized as we prepared to end the call.

"I guess you're too important to go on vacation," she laughed. I made the moment awkward with silence. After I hung up, I limped into the bathroom. This time, the pill made it all the way to my stomach.

∞

THE MEMORY DISSOLVED, and I was transported from Denver back to San Francisco. The meeting had disbanded, and I was seated at my desk, resting an open palm on my chest. The extra heartbeat was still there, palpable to the touch. I wrestled with my anxiety a moment before carrying it to Monica's office, where I poked my head in the door.

"I'm sorry to bother you, but I'm not feeling well. I'm short of breath, and my heart is beating funny."

"I'm sorry to hear that," she repeated her noncommittal phrase from earlier.

"I think I should see a doctor." I hoped she would urge me to take care of myself like she usually did.

"If that's what you think you need, then that's what you should do," she replied in a neutral tone. Guilt pricked my conscience.

"I'll complete a pass of the model and see how I feel before I decide what to do?" It was more of a question and less of a statement.

"That'd be helpful," the flood of Monica's relief made me sway on my feet. "Please let me know when you're done." I pressed my lips together and returned to my desk, where I slid my hand into the drawer. Checking to make sure no one was looking, I washed down two Percocet with leftover coffee. Since returning from the wedding, I'd grown expert at convincing doctors to feed my habit.

. . .

A COUPLE OF HOURS LATER, I faced Monica from her office door again.

"I'm leaving for urgent care."

"Darn, you looked so focused!" The gentle embrace of Percocet softened her disappointed reply. "I was hoping you felt better and could stay."

"I already made an appointment," I lied.

"Good luck, then. I hope we see you back after the weekend."

Sunshine broke through the remnants of fog as I descended into the BART station a few minutes later. Pressure built in my ears when the train shot into the Transbay Tube, deep under the waters of the San Francisco Bay. The feeling was usually no more than a nuisance; however, this time, nausea overcame me, and black spots danced in my vision. I panicked, certain this was the heart attack I expected. I grabbed the hand of the woman next to me.

"I'm telling you this in case I pass out," I rushed. "I've felt sick all day. When we entered the Tube, it got worse. If something happens, please call 911 and tell them I think it might be a heart attack." She studied my face.

"Girl, you better not faint in here!" My heart raced, and cold sweat beaded on my forehead. I dropped my head between my knees. A man's voice spoke into a two-way wall speaker.

"There's a woman in this car who says she thinks she's having a heart attack!"

"Please stand by her," the operator's reply crackled. "We'll stop at Lake Merritt for emergency personnel to board." The man came to stand in the aisle next to me. I kept my head down, studying his scuffed wingtips. As we pulled into the station, I looked up to watch the paramedics rushing the platform. Everything faded to black.

WHEN I CAME TO, a uniformed EMT squatted in front of me, peering into my face.

"Hello there! Welcome back," he sung out. I tensed my body to stand. "Take it slow, ma'am," he held me down by my shoulders. A blood pressure cuff squeezed my arm, and I remembered what had happened.

Despite having my wish for another panic attack granted, I argued, "I'm fine! I just fell asleep." The EMT's eyebrows arched up.

"We received a call that you might be having a heart attack, and you were unconscious when we arrived. We want to help."

"Please let me go," I begged. "I'll be fine!" A second EMT flanked me.

"Until we determine what caused your symptoms, ma'am, we can't leave you," he explained as they half-carried me off the train and laid me on a gurney.

While the ambulance crawled in pre-holiday traffic, my mind raced. What if something's really wrong with me? What if we have to postpone the party? What if my mom finds out? In a rush, I remembered Ed. He had no idea what was happening. I started texting, declining the call when his face popped up.

"I'll be okay," I tapped out. "I just fainted. They're taking me to the ER out of an abundance of caution."

"What about the party? And your mom?"

"DO NOT tell my mom anything! I'll text when I know more."

IT WAS late afternoon when I was finally ensconced in a sterile hospital room, where I wasted no time ringing the bedside buzzer. A red-haired woman zipped in.

"How can I help, honey?"

"I'm recovering from surgery, and my knee got jostled during the ambulance ride. May I please have something to help with the pain?"

"Of course. What do you take?"

"Percocet, ten milligrams," I watched her trace a red pen down my chart. "I usually take two when the pain is bad like this."

"When was your last dose?"

"Oh, gosh, I don't know. It's been weeks. My knee doesn't hurt most of the time." An alarm sounded in the corridor.

"Hold tight, honey. I'll get it in a minute," the nurse said, shoving my chart back on the hook at the foot of the bed. When she ran out, I pounced on the buzzer again and replayed my request to the blonde woman who responded.

"Be right back," she scribbled with her red pen. A few minutes later, she reappeared, carrying a lone round pill in a tiny paper ramekin. It was half the dose I was angling for, but I swallowed it with water from a flimsy pink cup and thanked her. I was resting with my eyes closed when the red-headed nurse bustled in ten minutes later, surprising me with an identical ramekin and an apologetic air. She tipped its contents onto my palm. There were two pills this time.

"It got crazy out there, but I finally broke away," she smiled warmly. I bit the inside of my cheek while she flipped through my chart. "Oh, look, I marked it as dispensed when I was in here before," she laughed. I tipped my pink cup in salute to her and washed the extra doses down.

At five o'clock, the orderly arrived to take me for an EKG and bloodwork. At six o'clock, Ed and I texted some more, agreeing that he'd take the kids to do party errands. At seven o'clock, just as I was considering requesting another round of painkillers, the doctor pushed open my door.

"Mrs. Black," he said formally. "You had a scare today. I understand you were seen in an emergency room last month for the same symptoms?"

"Yes," I'd spent the empty hours plotting precisely what to say when the doctor arrived. I launched into my speech. "That doctor diagnosed a panic attack, but I'm certain he was wrong! These symptoms are not a figment of my imagination. I don't have panic attacks. There's more to it..." I trailed off. I could feel him waiting to talk instead of listening to me.

"Uh-huh, I understand," his absent reply proved he'd ignored my words. "Look, I'm going to be direct with you. You are morbidly obese, and it is killing you. Although your EKG was normal and your blood counts

31

are within acceptable ranges, they're not going to stay like that forever. I see you have a history of gestational diabetes—"

"That is totally resolved!" I burst out. Diagnosed in my second pregnancy, I'd injected insulin every night until Elsie was born. Afterward, I skipped all of my endocrinology appointments. Ignorance was better than the shame of being told I had Type II diabetes.

"—and women who have gestational diabetes have an elevated incidence of developing Type II within ten years of delivery," the doctor finished as if I hadn't interrupted. "Once you're armed with more knowledge about diet, exercise, and the damage you're doing to your body, I'm confident you'll commit to saving your own life by losing weight."

"Okay," my tone made it clear his advice was unwelcome. He sat back on his stool.

"You have two young kids, don't you?"

"Yes."

"Don't you want to be around for their graduations? Their weddings?" His questions called up another memory. This time, I was a chunky twelve-year-old, perched on a barstool, alone in a yellow Arizona kitchen. The princess phone shrilled.

"Hello?"

"Hi, Pal! It's your Dad and Charlie." My dad never called without his girlfriend on the line anymore. I liked Charlie, and she was only eleven years older than me.

They'd been dating since he moved to New York after my parents' divorce. "We have something to tell you. We're getting married!"

"That's exciting!" I gasped.

"The wedding is next May," Charlie said. "Will you be a junior bridesmaid?"

"Yes!" We chatted about dress colors and styles before saying goodbye.

A couple of months later, when I visited my dad, Charlie and I were measured by a seamstress. Much to my embarrassment, the wedding shop ordered a women's size for me. Charlie fretted the whole drive home, lamenting her dress size, which was half of mine.

Back in Arizona, I received another call. This time, Dad was solo on the line.

"How're you doing, Pal?" he asked. "Tripping around and having fun?"

"Yeah, I made a friend named Audra. She likes to skateboard, like me!" My mom and I had relocated from the sprawling ranch house with the yellow kitchen, where we'd lived as a family, to a smaller house in another city. Until Audra came looking for me after seeing me skateboard past her house, I'd been lonely and dreading the start of seventh grade, friendless in a new school district.

"Skateboarding is good exercise! Have you been swimming laps every day, too?"

"Audra and I are tanning with baby oil. We want to be super dark when school starts!" He adopted the tone of a game show host with his next words.

"Listen, Pal; I have an exciting offer for you!" My

defenses shot up, as they did at any quixotic change in his mood. "You're going into junior high, and pretty soon you'll go to high school. You don't want to turn into an overweight teenager. You'll never be able to lose any of the weight you're gaining if you get too old. I'll pay you five dollars a pound for every pound you lose before the end of the year. There's no limit on how much I'll pay!" As he talked, I pressed a salty fingertip into a patch of raw flesh at the corner of my thumbnail. It stung, but it didn't match the pain of his words. I dug in hard. Searing agony traveled up my arm, through my elbow and shoulder, into my heart. "How does that sound?"

"That sounds great," I lied. All I could think about was making a German pancake with apple pie filling.

"You don't sound enthusiastic, Pal. Five dollars a pound is a lot, but I'm willing to go higher. How about ten dollars a pound? That's even better! Just think, that's a hundred bucks for every ten pounds you lose!"

"Okay," I would agree to anything if it meant I could hang up. "I have to go, Audra is here," I lied. After we said goodbye, I pulled out the ingredients to make my snack in a 9" x 9" pan. I ate it all.

THE MEMORY FADED. I was still in the ER, still facing the doctor who wanted to blame my weight without hearing anything I had to say.

"You owe it to your kids to lose weight and get

healthy," he pressed. I'd acted out this play before. It was time to assume my guilty role.

"I want to lose weight, but it's been so tough recovering from surgery! My knee still hurts, which keeps me from exercising much," I infused my voice with an invitation for him to help me. He thumbed through my chart.

"I see prescriptions here for three different painkillers."

"Yes, but I don't have any left." He kept reading.

"You also have sleep apnea. With complications like apnea and panic attacks, I'm uncomfortable prescribing more than ten pills. Return to your orthopedic surgeon if the pain is keeping you from normal activity." A sigh of irritation escaped my lips at the same time a notification sounded on my phone.

"Done with party errands," the text read. "Coming to the hospital."

"Is everything okay?" the doctor asked.

"My husband and kids are coming to the hospital."

"That works out beautifully since I'm about to discharge you." A frisson of panic zinged in my chest.

"I'm not ready to go home!"

"You're not in immediate danger. I wouldn't discharge you if I thought otherwise." I couldn't stop my fears from tumbling out.

"I *know* something's wrong with me! My heart jumps all over, and my arms fall asleep for no reason. My job is so stressful! I can't sleep or concentrate on anything. We're hosting a party tomorrow. I *know* I'm going to go home and have a heart attack!" The doctor's face grew stony as he listened.

"Go home and cancel your plans for the weekend. Make the follow-up appointments I'm ordering. If you don't change the way you treat your body, you'll die much sooner rather than later." At his rebuke, my mind slipped into paranoid overdrive. I imagined myself keeling over dead at the party or facing arrest for lying about opioid prescriptions. The downward spiral of my thoughts halted when he asked a question I'd heard before. "Have you ever been in talk therapy with a trained psychotherapist?"

"No, why?"

"A therapist can teach you how to manage stress, which will help you lose weight. Losing weight is the headline here, and you need all the help you can get," he stood and slipped his pen into the pocket of his white coat. "The admin nurse will be in shortly to send you on your way. Please take care of yourself."

Alone again, I picked at my scabbed cuticles till they bled. The nurse arrived at the same time as another text from Ed.

"We're here."

THIRTY MINUTES LATER, I faced the doors that would belch me into the waiting area. I was weighed down with my briefcase and worry. And a gnawing hunger for more Percocet. This hospital hadn't filled the prescription. When the doors parted, Elsie leaped into my arms. Eddie followed close behind, burying his face in my waist with his mouth running a mile a minute.

"Mommy! I was so scared when Daddy said you were in the hospital again! Are you okay?"

"Yes, I'm okay. Please don't worry."

"What happened?"

"I was on a BART train with broken air conditioning. It got too hot, and I fainted. It scared the other passengers, so I got to ride in an air-conditioned ambulance instead of the crowded train!" I tried to make it sound like an adventure.

"It's hot. I want ice cream, so I don't faint!" Elsie chimed in. She and Eddie started squabbling about dessert.

Ed came close by my side. His face was guarded, seeking reassurance that all was indeed well. I tightened my lips into a smile shape that I hoped was convincing. He pulled me against his chest with one arm, and we shared a family hug before separating and walking, all four hand-in-hand, to the parking lot.

CHAPTER 4

*A*fter loading the kids in the car, Ed and I stood outside to talk.

"Do you want to get your car now?" he asked.

"Yeah, there's too much to do before the party tomorrow." In my head, I added, "*...and I want my pills tonight!*" Ed was still talking.

"...Costco had avocados, so I bought the ingredients for guacamole."

"What?"

"The avocados were ripe. I already texted Brian to tell him." Our friend Brian loved to dip party foods in guacamole, going as far as to frost sugar cookies with it once.

"It's too much work to make guacamole."

"I'll help you make it," he bargained. "I can chop the ingredients and mix it if you tell me the proportions."

"You already have jobs to do."

"I can make guacamole and clean up the yard, Shell!" My impatience boiled over.

"Why do you do this? You promise things, hand them off to me, and I have to figure out how to get them done, or else everyone is let down!"

"Stop pre-criming me! I told you I'd help make the guac, and that's what I'll do." I pressed my lips together and slammed the passenger door. Ed settled in the driver's seat. I thought about telling him what the doctor said, canceling the party, admitting I needed his help. I was ready to ask for it. I took a breath.

My lips wouldn't unlock.

I couldn't do it. I was afraid of bringing on a full-fledged fight, of disappointing our friends, of appearing less-than-perfect. I gnawed at my raw cuticles until Ed parked beside my car.

"See you at home?"

"I'm stopping at the pharmacy for a prescription. You go home and put the kids to bed. I have to get up extra early now that I have to make guacamole!" My sarcasm lacked starch, sounding apathetic instead of angry.

Twenty minutes later, idling in the pharmacy parking lot, I shook out two pills and stared at them in the semidarkness. I swallowed the tsunami of self-hate that towered in my chest. The pills followed with stale water from a bottle pried out of the rear footwell. Scowling at my reflection in the rearview mirror, I spoke aloud.

"The pills aren't in control, idiot. You are. You're quitting this nonsense before you go to Hawaii!" It wasn't the first time I'd drawn a line in the sand for myself. I narrowed my eyes. "In fact, this is your final weekend. You're quitting Monday!"

At home, I changed into droopy pajamas and brushed my teeth. I watched my hands pry open a bottle of OxyContin as if disconnected from them. I giggled to myself, thinking, *This is like the day before a new diet. Gotta load up on the good stuff!"*

Ed was reading when I floated into the space between the sheets. He rolled toward me, belly coming to rest against my arm as I stared at the ceiling, enjoying waves of vertigo.

"Are you feeling better?" he asked.

"Much better, thanks. I took a Percocet." When he advanced, I hesitated. Kissing back was easier than talking about my feelings. Ten minutes later, he lifted his head from between my knees.

"What's wrong?"

"Nothing."

"I can tell something's wrong," he said. I couldn't stop worrying about whether my body would cooperate. I'd spent hours what-iffing this recent frigidity, wondering if it were early menopause or C-section scarring.

"It's probably the Percocet. It makes me feel a bit numb." Oblivious to my unspoken wish that he give up, he dove down with renewed enthusiasm.

"I don't think it's going to work tonight," I pushed at him with a knee. "You should enjoy yourself, though." He lay back.

"Are you sure?"

"Yes." I climbed on top. When he finished, I rolled back to my side of the bed and erected a wall of pillows between us in my nightly ritual. I built the wall because he slept warm, complaining if I crowded him under the covers, and because I hated the feeling of his breath blowing on me.

Long after Ed began snoring, I stared at the ceiling, pleading with my brain to let me sleep. I finally grabbed my phone. Playing through Words With Friends turns, I responded here and there to a chat comment. A notification popped up.

"You have a new challenge from Lydia! Accept, Decline, Block?" The name ignited the memory of a time eight years earlier when I was 31.

THE SOUNDS of happy hour in the lobby bar of San Jose's Hotel De Anza swirled around. We sat close together on a red velvet couch sipping wine, and getting to know each other.

"Why'd you get your second tattoo?" Lydia asked.

"To celebrate the closing of my first investment banking deal."

"Show it to me."

"It's in the middle of my back. I can't exactly show you right now!"

"Come on! No one's looking." My insides melted at the way her smoky voice whispered the coercion.

"All right, but you don't get to see the first one I

got," I teased, slipping my fingers into the hem of my sweater. I tugged up. Lightning raced in my veins when she touched my skin.

"Is this it?" she breathed the unnecessary question into my ear.

"Yes," I croaked.

"Mmmmm, I like it!" Her fingers stroked back and forth. I held perfectly still, but my thoughts flew fast. I must be gay! A woman's touch wouldn't feel this good if I were straight. "Are you going to get more tattoos?" she asked.

"Yes, but I don't have anything in mind right now." Lydia's fingers, which had continued tracing circles over the lizards on my back, curved around the sensitive skin at my waist. Her lips stirred my hair.

"Do you want to get a room upstairs?"

IN BED, beside my sleeping husband, I came with a gasp. The memory faded. I was sore when I pulled my fingers away. I checked the clock. It had taken almost a half-hour and left me further from sleep than ever. I kicked off the covers and twisted around to squash a pillow between my knees. I wondered where Lydia was now. I wondered if she remembered me. I thought about taking another pill. I must have slept because, sometime in the early morning hours, a familiar dream unfolded.

I found myself buckled in a seat in a pressurized cabin. Every detail was utterly clear and realistic, down to the compacted Berber carpet on the floor and the dog-eared emergency card tucked into the pocket facing me. Without warning, the plane plummeted. People and personal items levitated then dropped when the pilot regained control.

"Thank you, Jesus!" yelled a fellow passenger.

"Someone, please! We need help over here!" Amidst the wails of the injured, oxygen masks popped out of the ceiling.

"Folks," the captain's voice intoned, "we're cleared for an emergency landing at the closest airfield. Please stay calm and follow crew instructions. I promise everything's going to be fine." A loud boom rocked the plane, and we tipped into a slow nose dive. As the fuselage began its death rattle, untethered bodies and luggage pin-balled around me. I strained to disappear, tightening my core like a steel corset. The earth closed in through the window. I began chanting in my sleep.

"I don't belong here. This is not real. This is not happening to me!" Everything went blank. I knew I escaped before the plane crashed, but I could never see how! I was momentarily paralyzed, awake inside a frozen shell, waiting for my brain and body to reconnect.

When I could control my arms, I shook Ed.

"What if the plane crashes when we fly to Hawaii?"

"Huh?" he struggled awake.

"What if the plane crashes!"

"The plane isn't going to crash."

"There haven't been any big plane crashes recently. It seems like the world is due."

"Shell, you have a statistics degree, so you know there's no correlation. Why are you awake?"

"I can't sleep. I'm worried."

"There's nothing to worry about. Think of it this way. If the plane crashes, there's absolutely nothing you can do about it." I took a deep breath.

"I dreamed about a plane crash," I owned the truth. His silhouette, propped on an elbow across the bed from me, slouched.

"Oh. Is that what this is about?"

"Yes!"

"Your dreams aren't real, Shell."

"I *know* it's real! I just know it," I insisted.

"You also think your dreams about me doing things I've never done are real, and you wake up mad at me for them. One time, you were mad at me for two whole days for something you *dreamt*." I flinched. "You'll be fine in the morning. Good night." He flopped on his side, facing away from me. I put my back toward his and smothered my sobs.

The family room TV blared. My eyes opened to broad daylight. Eddie wasn't shy about turning on cartoons for himself and his sister when their parents slept in. I scrabbled for my phone and yelled. Ed jumped.

"What happened?"

"It's after eleven! We're never going to be ready for the party on time!" We were both already upright and throwing on clothes.

"Let's get started," Ed said. "I'll give the kids jobs in the yard."

As they worked outside, I slammed around the kitchen. Between stirring onion dip and rolling tortilla wraps, the avocados in their green mesh bags caught my eye. I'd forgotten about the guacamole. Pins and needles prickled.

"Eddie!" I yelled. The patio screen went *swish-ka-chunk*. He trotted in.

"Yes, Mom?"

"Tell your father to come here, please." I waited, arms and legs crossed, resting my butt against the counter. Another *swish-ka-chunk* heralded his return.

"Dad can't come in. He's fixing Roy." Roy was our pet name for the pool cleaner robot. I followed Eddie to the screen door.

"What's wrong with Roy?" I called.

"He keeps getting stuck," Ed called back.

"We're just going to take him out when the guests are here. You need to come make the guacamole."

"I'll be there in a minute," he balked. Without warning, my anxiety slammed into overdrive.

"Take care of Roy later! I need your help now!" Something he heard in my voice made Ed come to face me through the screen door.

"Don't worry, Shell. We'll get everything done," he soothed as he led me to the kitchen where he sliced into the red onion. As we worked side-by-side, I repeated all the details of the day, from what time to start cooking to when we would light fireworks. I couldn't stop worrying that something was going to happen that would ruin the party. Ed reassured me that the decisions we'd already settled on were still the best ones. Eddie and Elsie came in.

"We're done scooping poop," Eddie said.

"We want to swim," Elsie added.

"Daddy and I have to make food, so you have to wait until the party." Elsie looked interested.

"I want to be a chef! What can I make?"

"Wash your hands," I sent them off and consulted Ed. "Do you think they can handle the pigs-in-a-blanket?" He was halfway through chopping the onions, knife slack in his hand.

"Sure! That's easy." I popped a refrigerated dough can against the edge of the counter. He grabbed it along with a cutting board. "I'll set them up in the dining room." When the kids reappeared, I handed Eddie a package of smoked sausages and cookie sheets.

"Give these to Daddy. Let him show you how."

"I know how!" Elsie said proudly. A few minutes later, Ed cranked the stereo. 'Start Me Up' by the Rolling Stones echoed through the house. It began to feel like a party. From my apron pocket, I withdrew my first two pills of the day. They disappeared with a pint of orange juice. My cell rang.

"Hi, Mom!"

"Hi, honey. We got on the road this morning at about eight o'clock. We'll be there between four and five."

"Great! You'll probably arrive when we're on our tenth pitcher of margaritas," I joked, thoughtlessly triggering her fear of missing out.

"You can't start the party without us," she said to me before she started yelling over the mouthpiece. "Matt, I told you we should have left earlier!"

"Mom!" I wanted to retract what I said, but I could hear my stepdad's garbled annoyance in the background. "Mom! We'll still be partying when you get here! You won't miss anything. Ed and I—" I stalled mid-sentence. Through the kitchen window, I saw Ed backing out in my car. I pulled the phone away and inspected the screen. Nothing. I returned it to my ear.

"Is the yard ready?" my mom asked. I stifled a groan.

"Ed's out back right now. In fact, I need to go help him."

"Okay, I can't wait to hug you!"

"Love you. Bye."

"Wait! WAIT!"

"What, Mom?"

"Do you need anything from Costco?"

"You don't need to go to Costco. We have a ton of food."

"We don't like the choices you have for breakfast at your house."

"I'm going now," I hung up and dialed Ed. He didn't answer. I phoned again, fury at his disappearance eclipsing vexation from my mom's call.

"Hello?" he finally answered.

"Where'd you go?"

"I'm getting plywood to put under the fireworks." This chore was not on my list.

"What's wrong with you? Now is not the time to do

47

that!" A hysterical sob seized my throat. "I can't do all this by myself, Ed. Get back here right now, or we won't have the party!" Eddie and Elsie listened from the doorway. They started talking over each other.

"Mommy, are you okay?"

"Is Daddy okay?"

"Are we having the party?"

"Go to your rooms!" I yelled. Into the phone, I growled, "You come home now," and hung up without waiting for an answer. I marched down the hall toward the bedrooms. Elsie was playing with dolls on her floor when I walked by. Eddie, in the next room, was face down on his bed. I paused.

"Eddie, stop crying. Everything's alright." He lifted his head.

"Why are you mad at Daddy?"

"I'm not. You need to stop eavesdropping on my phone conversations."

"I'm sorry. Is Daddy coming home?"

"Yes, he's on his way." His face brightened.

"Elsie and I finished putting the piggies on the trays, come see!"

"Get Elsie and meet me there," I instructed before continuing down the hall to the master bedroom, into the master bathroom, and into the medicine cabinet. I stared at the bottles. I had two strengths of Norco from which to choose. I took one of the lower dosage pills and headed back to the kitchen.

After I approved their handiwork with the hors d'oeuvres, the kids watched me push a cookie sheet into the oven. We all peered out the front window at the empty driveway. The nightmare plane crash feeling overtook me.

"I guess I have to make the guacamole since your father isn't rushing home to take care of his commitments!"

"You said Daddy was coming home," Eddie looked worried. I regretted my outburst.

"Don't worry, he is." Elsie, already a shrewd observer of character, inspected my face.

"It sounds like you're mad at Daddy," she said. I took up the knife next to the abandoned pile of onions.

"I'm not. It must be the onions. Onions make your throat feel funny, and sometimes they make you cry. Go get the inflatables ready." They raced away. I finished chopping onions. Next, I chopped tomatoes, cilantro, and peppers. I cut the avocados and limes in half. Ed pulled up, unloaded the plywood, and breezed in.

"Hey, sorry that took so long," his eye caught the neat piles of vegetables on my cutting board. "Ready for me to make the guacamole?"

"No! *I'm* making the guacamole!"

"I promised you I'd mix it. At least let me do that."

"You go do *your* jobs. The ones you agreed to *before* you bought the avocados!" He left. When the doorbell rang twenty minutes later, I was in the bathroom, taking one of the higher-dosage Norco tabs. It was party time.

CHAPTER 5

*W*hile Ed took drink orders from arriving guests, I replayed the tale of my ER visits to my friend Cathy. Her son and Eddie had been best friends since preschool. As the boys' friendship grew over the years, so did the closeness between our families. That is until Ed and I allowed other parents to influence us to exclude them from a kids' sports team we co-founded. We regretted our actions and apologized, but the relationship never fully recovered. Cathy listened patiently to my long, drawn-out story.

"...none of the doctors can figure out the constellation of symptoms. A new one pops up every day!"

"I'm sure that's scary. You should've let me and Dan know what was going on last night when you were at the hospital. We could've picked up the kids and fed them." I felt my face flush.

"You're nicer to us than we deserve." Cathy waved off my apologetic tone.

"It's all water under the bridge. Our kids are what's important. Dan and I love your kids. We'd do anything we could to help them." Ed joined us in the kitchen.

"Margarita time!" he announced. I was thankful for the interruption.

"Can you please set the margarita machine up on the other side of the kitchen?" I requested.

"I'm using the VitaMix."

"No, remember? We decided to use the Margaritaville thing today."

"It takes more ice than we have. If you want to use it, I'll have to go get some." The fact that we needed bags of ice had somehow escaped my list. I wavered. I didn't want him to go anywhere, even for party supplies, but I was tired of answering 'no, not yet' when my mom asked whether we'd used her gift. Dan walked up and put his arm around Cathy's shoulders.

"What's up with the margaritas?" he asked.

"We have to get ice," Ed answered. "Let's take Jerry and Masa!" The decision was made for me. When they screeched down the street, I started to worry. What if he crashed the car? What if someone drowned while he was gone? What if my heart attack happened now? Cathy saw me frowning.

"Don't worry, Shell. I'll help. The guys need a little time out." As we mixed drinks, I itched to talk about my nightmare, but I was afraid Cathy would react the same way Ed had. I remembered a rule at work that required high-level officers of the company to book separate flights when flying to the same destination, then used it to lead the conversation without mentioning my dream.

"We found out we have to change our flights to Hawaii."

"So soon before your trip! What happened?"

"Our life insurance company is making Ed and me fly separately." Cathy, who was a legal secretary, looked skeptical but asked exactly what I wanted her to ask.

"Why would an insurance company care if you were on the same plane?"

"Because they don't want to pay on both policies if we die in the same plane crash."

"I never heard of that for regular people before!" Jade, another friend who'd joined us, chimed in. "How'd they find out about your vacation?" This was not the direction I wanted the discussion to go, but I couldn't ignore her.

"I got it in my head that work would interfere with the trip, so I called to ask if they offer vacation insurance. Apparently, my call raised warning bells." Jade had more questions.

"What if they never found out and the plane crashed? Would they still pay?" Painted into a corner of my own making, I fled my friends' confused stares, stopping in the backyard to drain another Tequila Sunrise. Alcohol and painkillers swirled in my stomach, mixing into a shame cocktail. Elsie grabbed my hand.

"Momma! Are you going to swim with us? You promised!" Cheers erupted when I lined up with the kids at the deep end of the pool. I felt myself sway when I was about to dive in and had to pause to catch my balance. A tiny girl stood beside me.

"Why are you so fat?" she asked, staring up, awestruck.

"Sierra, we don't call people fat," her mother, sitting nearby, reprimanded. "That's rude. Apologize to Elsie's mommy!" I felt the little girl's confusion. Now she could barely look at me.

"I'm sorry, Elsie's mommy."

"Sticks and stones may break my bones," I chanted as my mom had taught me when I was little, "but words will never hurt me!" I dove in and surfaced amidst a group of older kids trying to organize a game, thankful the water obscured my fat body.

"Want to make a wave pool?" I asked. I loved to jump up and down, crouching underwater, then firing myself upward like a giant piston until waves crashed over the edge onto the deck. "Ryder, stand there. Lila, you get in the deeper part. Everyone jump!" I tried to siphon off the excitement around me, willing the childish laughter to erase my bleakness.

At the apex of a jump, I spied Sierra and Elsie clinging to the edge of the pool. Their small bodies were incapable of navigating the breakers. Panicking, I dove under and kicked my way to them. By the time I arrived, Sierra's mother was reaching down to pluck Sierra out of harm's way. She shot me a dirty look before turning on her heel and carrying her daughter to safety.

Where Sierra's mother had stood a moment earlier,

my mother now loomed. A perfect foot-high wave escaped the coping and soaked her shoes as she looked down at me, trying to protect my daughter from the self-created tempest.

"Michelle, what are you doing?" she asked.

"Swimming," I answered sheepishly.

Elsie tried to hoist herself over the edge, calling out, "Grams, watch me dive!" A wave threw her back against my chest.

Eddie spied his grandmother and shouted excitedly, "Grams, you're here!" A wave slapped his open mouth. He sputtered and coughed. I panicked again, fearing my mom's disapproval.

"STOP! Everyone out," my voice rang across the backyard. "No more swimming! Out! OUT!" The flagstone pool deck was an inch deep in water. Kids scrambled to stand at the edge and regarded me with wary eyes. Ed and my stepdad came around the corner lugging bags of ice and took in the scene.

"Shell, is everything okay?" Ed asked. I wanted to bawl, *"No! Nothing is okay!"* but Cathy, whom I hadn't noticed hovering, rescued me.

"Everyone, take a five-minute break!" she called out. "When you come back, the waves will be gone, and I can time races." I avoided her eyes, pushing Elsie onto the deck. Before Ed could ask anything more, I jumped on him.

"Have you made the margaritas yet?"

"No, we just got back," he put his arm around my mom's shoulder and squeezed. "Can you believe how fast Grams and Pop got here today?" I toweled off as they chatted.

"How's my favorite son-in-law?" she teased.

"Your only son-in-law, you mean," Ed bantered, and they laughed together. "Did you remember to bring Matt's computer?" He had offered to update my stepdad's PC during their visit.

"The minivan is full of computer stuff. I even brought the cables!"

"Grams brought everything and two kitchen sinks!" my stepdad chimed in. Laughter eased the tension in the aftermath of my wave pool.

"Can you help me get the food ready?" I asked my mom.

"Give me one minute. I have gifts for Cathy and Jade." My mom crocheted kitchen washcloths and towel toppers while she watched TV. She had more TV time than friends, so her generosity extended to my friends. She moved off, calling out to my stepdad, "Matt, I need help getting something out of the van."

Feeling mutinous, I made my way to the kitchen. My mom stuck her head in after me.

"Why don't you go change while I give the gifts?" she suggested.

"I don't need to change."

"You're wearing a wet swimsuit. You don't want it to make you itchy, and you shouldn't cook in that flimsy material."

"It'll dry in a minute, and I'm nowhere near an open flame."

"Shelley," she checked to be sure we were alone and dropped her voice, "it isn't appropriate for you to be walking around in that suit."

"What's wrong with it?" I challenged.

"It isn't very flattering," she evaded.

"*How* is it not flattering?" I wanted her to say what she meant.

"You've gained some weight around your midsection," she gesticulated to my lower half. "And that suit is not covering everything up. Plus, with boobs like yours and mine, you need a suit with a built-in underwire bra!" I'd already tried to buy a new swimsuit twice that summer. I needed one for our impending trip to Hawaii, but I couldn't stomach looking at myself in the changing room mirrors. I'd abandoned both attempts in tears.

"No one gives a shit what I look like, Mother," I bit out.

"Denise, what are you doing?" my stepdad bellowed from the front door.

"Hold your horses, Matt," she yelled back before stepping closer to me. "This isn't decent in front of your guests," she insisted. I gave her my best pig-eyed stare, jaw jutting in defiance.

"I'm not waiting anymore!" Matt shouted. She followed his voice.

I retreated to exchange the offensive swimsuit for shorts and an XXL T-shirt. The shirt was tight in the chest, so I drew my arms inside and used my elbows to stretch it until the seams popped in protest. In the bathroom, I gave my reflection a talking-to.

"After you get back from Hawaii, you go to the gym at lunch every single day, you disgusting blob. No excuses!" I looked like my dad, except my glare was green instead of blue. I jumped when Ed tried to open the door.

"Shell, are you in here?"

"Don't come in!"

"When are you bringing the meat outside?"

"Is the grill ready?"

"It needs a little more time."

"How much more time?" I asked. When he hesitated, I followed with, "Have you started the charcoal yet?"

"No," he confessed. Anguish, far out of proportion to the situation, engulfed me. True to my premonition, the party was turning into a disaster. A dense pit formed in my stomach.

"Go get the charcoal ready!" I moaned. When I tried to find my dad's face in the mirror again, only I was there, shiny with sweat and smelling of chlorine. I looked stressed. Twenty-nine Xanax lurked under the sink.

BACK IN THE thick of the party, I poured myself another drink. Brian was entertaining a small crowd in the breakfast nook. He held something under the chocolate fountain.

"Shelley," Masato called to me. "Brian has a guac-stuffed brownie bite under the fountain. That's messed up!" More guests crowded in to see what the fuss was about.

"Brian, you're gonna puke," Dan teased.

"Does this well-oiled eating machine look like it ever puked? I didn't get this way overnight. I have skills!" Brian carried twenty years' worth of fat layered over a State Champion wrestler's frame and talked frankly about being overweight. I probed him with my empath sense, trying to learn the self-acceptance that eluded me. Ed walked in.

"How's the guac, Brian?"

"The best. You better catch up, son!" They went head-to-head with guacamole-dipped foods, like an Old West shootout. When the bowl was empty, Ed raised his arms in defeat.

"Too bad we didn't make more guacamole!" he laughed.

"Too bad *you* didn't make *any*!" I spat. Everyone looked vaguely uncomfortable. Brian cleared his throat.

"Everything's better with guac, and Michelle's is the best guac in the world. I should know, I travel hundreds of thousands of miles a year for work. Everywhere I go, I try the guacamole. There's none on the face of this planet better than Michelle's!" The compliment was excessive yet sincere in a way only Brian could pull off. Laughter rippled through the crowd. I had to laugh, too, or risk looking like an even bigger jerk than I already did. I stumbled as I finished loading the meat tray. My mom eyed me with concern.

"Is your knee okay?"

"Yes, it's fine."

"You stumbled like you're drunk."

"I'm not drunk!"

"Why are you so uptight? This is a party."

"You would be uptight, too, if you spent last night —" I stopped. I hadn't told my mom about either of my ER visits, and I'd sworn Ed to secrecy on the matter.

"You're so wound up, no one's going to enjoy being around you," she warned. I shoved a stack of BBQ tools at her.

"Carry these and follow me," I sighed, hoisting the giant platter of meat.

After we delivered our payload to Ed, who was tending the glowing charcoal, I cast about for something to do. The food was laid out. Everyone had drinks. No one was asking anything of me, yet, I could not relax. Instead of inducing calm, the Xanax made it harder to think. I paced through the party, chanting to myself, *"I want this to be over! Please be over!"* My cell rang.

"Hey, Liesl," I greeted my best friend from college.

"Happy Fourth!"

"Same to you. What're you guys up to today?"

"We're having a family BBQ, then watching neighborhood fireworks. How's your party?"

"Brian and Ed already ate all the guacamole," I groused.

"That doesn't surprise me," she chuckled. "Hey, have you paid the deposit for the cruise?" Our families were planning a joint Disney Cruise the next summer. The pit, still sitting in my stomach from earlier, swelled.

59

"Yes, we paid for our whole reservation." Technically, we'd maxed out a VISA on it.

"What stateroom did you get?" I hadn't spoken to her in over a month, but suddenly I wanted to hang up.

"I have it in the confirmation email. Can we talk when I'm back from Hawaii?"

"Sure! Tell your mom I love her."

"Okay, love you. Bye!" I slumped into a chair. I must have blacked out because the next thing I knew, Ed was standing in front of me. Grilled meat smells wafted around, and a buffet line was forming.

…blackout…

The party was going strong. Several couples danced in our living room. I clutched a giant margarita and shouted the words to the song Ed and I called ours.

"If you like piña coladas…" I sang.

"…and gettin' caught in the rain…" Ed joined me. His margarita spilled over the side of the glass when he went down on one knee as if to propose to me. I took his hand and kissed it, willing everyone to witness our perfect relationship.

…blackout…

I was crying in the bathroom, staring into a pill bottle.

…blackout…

I was yelling goodbye in the front yard. Cathy's kids raced past. She followed them and stopped to hug me.

"Thanks for having us," she said. Dan stumbled up behind her and wrapped his arms around her neck, nuzzling. "Obviously, Dan had a great time."

"I'm not drunk!" Dan insisted. Cathy and I laughed. Ed came around the corner.

"What's so funny?"

"Dan swears he's not drunk," I answered.

"Then, he better come over again this weekend and do it right!" Ed issued the invitation without meeting my eyes. The guys high-fived, nearly missing each other's palms. Praying she would say no, but fully expecting a yes, I looked at Cathy.

"Do you want to come over before the tournament?"

"No, I don't think so," her cold reply shook me. My empath sense was overwhelmed. I could feel her disapproval of my behavior and that she was barely tolerating being in my presence.

…blackout…

The only remaining guests other than family were our friends, Miguel and Masato. Miguel entertained my mom with stories of his mom's international business travels. Masa, always active and helpful, tidied the kitchen. I tried to help, but my brain couldn't seem to make my body finish a task. Masa pushed me aside and took over wrapping cold burger patties.

I went to hover near Ed, where he and my stepdad nursed margaritas at the kitchen table. Pop delivered the punchline of my favorite Ole & Lena joke.

"Well, Father, dey threw us outta Safeway!" Ed barked a laugh then stood.

"I'm down for the count. One too many margaritas!"

"Ed! You can't abandon me," I was frantic for him to stay put.

"Shell, I'm going to be sick," he lurched down the hall and out of sight.

…blackout…

Hugging my mom goodnight, I sobbed into her shoulder.

"I love you, my perfect daughter!" she crooned. I hated her calling me perfect. If I was perfect, I was never allowed to make a mistake.

…blackout.

CHAPTER 6

*O*pening my eyes the morning after the party was painful. Between my headache and hazy memories, I was afraid to face my family. I grabbed my phone to check the time and found three voicemails waiting. Reluctantly, I played them.

"Hi, Michelle. It's Monica. I came to the office to be on alert for the committee decision on the acquisition. They went in at 9 o'clock. Let's talk later." I hit delete.

"This is Violet calling from Dr. Drexler's office. She would like to schedule—" I hit delete. The final message was ten minutes old.

"This is your mother. I'm at Costco—" The phone vibrated in my hand.

"Hello?"

"I've been waiting for your callback," my mom greeted me.

"I just woke up."

"Do you want me to get crab legs?"

"No, I planned meals until we leave for the tournament."

"What about a rotisserie chicken for lunches?" My call waiting beeped.

"I need to answer the other line."

"The kids want Pub Mix. Is that okay?"

"Mom, I have to answer!" I clicked over.

"This is the endocrinology department. We'd like to set up your diabetes assessment. Is now a good time?"

"I'm on the other line. Can I return your call?" I listened to the number without taking it down. My mom was gone when I clicked back.

Wincing, I rolled out of bed to look for Ed. A two-foot stack of disembodied hard drives toppled when I pushed open the office door.

"Why are those there?"

"You're up! Did you sleep well?"

"I have a hangover," I complained. "You need to clean this office."

"The ER doc gave you pain meds for your knee, right? Those'll cure your hangover," he joked. "I'm about to hop on another call, but there's a break after, so I can eat lunch with everyone."

"If they were here, that'd be great."

"Oh, right. Your mom took the kids to Costco. You know how Elsie and Grams love shopping together." Thunderclouds gathered on my forehead.

"I hate it when my mom does this! I already planned the menu."

"It's no big deal. Freeze some of the stuff we bought before."

"Changing things makes more work for me," my anxiety, which simmered all the time now, began to boil.

"I'll help after my calls," Ed promised. I spun to leave and tripped on a computer case whose guts trailed across the rug.

"Clean this up!" I shrilled.

"It's on my list of things to do while you're at the tournament," he turned back to his computer.

Pressing my lips together, I retreated to the bathroom, cranked the shower, and took a Percocet. I longed for a Norco, too, but settled for a massive dose of ibuprofen and the billowing steam to ease my hangover. Spying mildew near the ceiling, I slapped at it with a wet washcloth till slimy green patches ran down the tile. The ancient fan had rusted to a standstill. We bought a new one, but, upon removing the crusty vent, beheld a rat's nest of wiring underneath. It joined our lengthy list of pending home improvement projects. The mildew circling the drain mesmerized me. I jumped when Elsie pounded on the door.

"Momma? Grams wants to know when you'll be done." I gritted my teeth, wishing people would stop banging on the bathroom door when I was inside.

"Tell her I'll be done when I'm done!"

When the hot water ran out, I followed laughter toward the backyard but stopped short. Tubs of snacks, two flats of bakery muffins, and a loaf of crusty bread crowded the kitchen counter. I swung open the refrigerator. Wedged between foil packets of party leftovers were crab legs and a rotisserie chicken. I shredded the handwritten menu on the front of the fridge and pulled out a clean sheet of paper. It was blank, and I was staring into space when Ed walked in.

"We wondered if you went back to bed," he commented.

"I don't know what to do with all this food," I spread my arms helplessly.

"Everyone else ate at Costco. What do you want for lunch?" Ed rummaged in a cabinet.

"The pantry is overflowing!"

"How about Hot Pockets?" he asked. I shook my head no and waited for him to return from the garage, where we kept a freezer full of Hot Pockets. A crash shook the kitchen. I guessed it was a dozen 2"x 4"s toppling from their precarious perch on a pile of plastic tubs that lined the single-track walkway wending through the bulging garage. When Ed reappeared, I confirmed.

"Lumber?"

"I know!" he blushed. "I need to get the garage cleaned up. Maybe Matt can help me with that."

"You need to fix his PC before you clean the garage," I warned. "My mom already asked when it'll be done." He started the microwave.

"Would you mind bringing my Hot Pockets to me? I need to hop on a call."

"I thought you were taking the afternoon off?"

"A customer issue emerged over the holiday."

"When will you be done?"

"Tonight or tomorrow. Gotta run," he slipped back into the office. I stared into space, waiting for the microwave to finish. After I served Ed's lunch, I wandered to the backyard. My mom was hanging wet towels while everyone else swam.

"There you are! We thought you went back to bed. I want to talk to you about last night."

"I don't need a lecture. I know I was drunk."

"That's not what I want to talk about, although, with the medications you use, I don't think you should drink so much."

"What do you mean, '*use*'?" I protested. She'd said it like it was a dirty word. "I take what's prescribed!"

"You brought up Wisconsin last night," she continued, ignoring my interruption. "I could tell what you said hurt Ed's feelings."

"So?"

"So, when we last talked about it, you said you were okay with your decision." An unhealed, three-year-old wound cracked open inside me.

"Why do you care more how Ed feels about Wisconsin than how I feel? I'm the one who missed a once-in-a-lifetime career opportunity!"

"You're my daughter, and your feelings are my first concern," her reassurance fell flat on my ears. "I happen to disagree that it was a good opportunity. It would've taken your family away from the security you have here, and farther away from me."

"You don't even know the whole story about Wisconsin!"

Confused, my mom said, "I only know what you told me, which is that you turned down the offer because Wisconsin was too far from good jobs for Ed, and there wouldn't be anything else for you if your job didn't work out. Is that true?" In my mind, I compared my mom's memory to my memory of what transpired three years earlier.

THE DEADLINE APPROACHED for me to accept a dizzyingly generous offer from a rival company. Their new CEO had been recruited from the same company as me, and I was one of only a few colleagues he'd tapped to join him. I'd already deferred my answer once.

After I put the kids to bed, I poked my head into the office and said, "We need to talk. Now." Ed followed me. I sat, arms and legs crossed, in one corner of a couch. He mirrored me in the exact opposite corner of the other couch, so we were as far apart as two people could be in the living room.

"What do you want to talk about?" The question irked me, but I wasn't about to be derailed.

"Are we in agreement that I'm going to accept Patrick's offer tomorrow?" He didn't answer. A few moments passed. I tried again. "This is the opportunity we've waited for. I let you take the lead when you had big chances. Now it's my turn!" This time, I let forty empty minutes tick past. I couldn't stand the silence anymore. "We have to make a decision. You can't just sit there and say nothing!" He finally spoke.

"I'm going to bed."

"I've been waiting all day to talk to you," I raged, following him. "You can't ignore me!"

"What do you want me to say?"

"I want you to answer me!" We retreated to our separate sides of the bed, and he lapsed into silence. I tried another tack.

"Ed, please. I want this with all of my heart, but I can't pick up and move to Wisconsin without you. Let's make this decision together. We've always talked about being a team." I waited. "Are you still awake?"

"Yes."

I cajoled and begged for hours, finally giving up at three a.m. He never said another word. At six o'clock, my alarm sounded. I knew he had not slept, just as I had not.

"Can we please make a decision?" I asked quietly. He rolled to look at me. Tears sprung to his eyes. I started crying, too. "What am I supposed to say to Patrick?"

"I don't know," he whispered. Soon it was five minutes past the deadline. Then ten. My sadness gave way to rancor when my phone rang.

"How can you refuse to make a decision? It isn't fair!" My phone rang again. The voicemail notification sounded. I played it on the speaker.

"Hi, Michelle. Just trying to get a hold of you. Call me back." I stared at Ed, focusing all the hope and impotence I felt. Minutes stretched out.

"I guess I have to call back," I finally snarled. Patrick picked up after a half-ring.

"Hey, Michelle." My heart hammered.

"I don't know how to say this. I can't accept your offer." It was Patrick's turn to be silent. "I'm sorry," I rushed to fill the emptiness. "This is my dream job. But I can't."

"Why?" Patrick's voice was hard. I felt I owed him the truth.

"My husband and I are unable to come to an agreement to move to Wisconsin." Patrick made an impatient sound. I'd witnessed him turn on people who wasted his time before.

"Good luck," he quipped. "You're gonna need it."

"Thank you for believing in me and giving me a chance."

"Goodbye, Michelle," the finality of his tone shut the door on our acquaintance. I dropped the phone. Ed listened to me sob for a moment before walking out. The memory faded.

∞

I REFOCUSED ON MY MOM, clutching a damp towel to her chest. Ashamed, I couldn't bring myself to tell her what really happened. She pressed on.

"I sensed at the time Ed didn't want to move to Wisconsin. You were so gung ho; maybe you didn't listen to him. You're lucky he's patient."

"This isn't about Wisconsin," I tried to explain. "I hate my job."

"Well, that's news to me. You said you were happy with Monica as your boss."

"Monica's a good boss, but being on the acquisition team is like having a second job! There's too much stress."

"Everyone's suffering in this economy. You're lucky you still have a job."

"Being unhappy with my career choice is unrelated to the economy," I argued.

"If you'd gone to Wisconsin, you'd be stuck doing finance for the rest of your life!" her voice rose.

"Maybe I would have liked it better working for Patrick!" The rise in my voice matched hers.

"In Wisconsin, you wouldn't have all the flexibility you have here with the kids," she pulled her trump card. "You said so yourself! Ed couldn't get a nearby job, so he'd be traveling all the time. You're lucky you have a husband who helps!" I couldn't take anymore scolding.

"Ed barely does what he agrees to, Mom! In addition to my two jobs at work, I have another full-time job here!"

"Everyone's marriage is like that," she dropped into a familiar rant. "It's the same with Pop and me. He never helps. If I don't tell him over and over again to empty the dishwasher or take out the trash, nothing gets done! That's just how men are. It was the same with my mom and dad. Nana always said Grandpère had no gumption and that someone in the family had to wear the pants." She focused on me. "I figured *you* wanted to wear the pants in your family, too." I struggled, afraid to admit I was unhappy with my choices. I took a deep breath. This was my mom; if I couldn't tell her, who could I tell?

"Maybe I used to want that, but not anymore."

"You can't change the rules now, Shelley!" I felt her

sudden terror, reflected in her harsh insistence. "Ed has his faults. So do you. At least he loves you and accepts your faults! You have to accept his, too. That's what marriage is!" The seeds of my mom's anxiety took hold and sprouted inside my chest, and I couldn't breathe.

"I have calls to make for work," I put an abrupt end to our talk.

"I thought you were on vacation today?"

"There's an acquisition starting, so I can't." I left her on the back porch, locked myself in the bedroom, took one big Norco and one little Norco, then laid down to wait. My phone rang long after the medicine took effect.

"Hi, Monica."

"We've got a challenge ahead. The committee said no to our acquisition proposal. Jay wants to prepare a rebuttal." My body reacted before she even asked, "Can you come into the office?"

"I was in the hospital Wednesday night. I'm resting on doctor's orders."

"Oh."

"I need to get going; one of the specialists is calling about a follow-up." Adrenaline coursed in my veins after I hung up. I lay back to catch my breath. The longer I stayed, the heavier my limbs grew, and the more impossible it seemed that I would ever stand again. An hour later, I dragged myself up. There was a note under the door.

"Took kids to park. Back in time for dinner. Love, Mom."

All afternoon I cleaned up the party mess and ran laundry, stacking basket after basket of dry clothes in the office. Each time I deposited one, Ed, who'd promised to fold between calls, said, "Thanks! I'll get to it soon."

Vast expanses of the day disappeared into opioid amnesia. When dinnertime rolled around, I confronted the refrigerator. Rewriting the menu had proven an insurmountable task. The kids and grandparents spilled through the front door while I stared into the abyss of blue-white light.

"Let's go to Red Robin," I said to my mom, who stood beside me.

"There's no reason to go out! We have a lot of food." I kept staring into the fridge. My decision-making process had ground to a halt.

"I don't know what to make," I sighed.

"Reheat leftovers," she counseled. Ed would object to leftovers, and I didn't feel like fighting him.

"I'm not in the mood for leftovers."

"You spend a lot going out to eat," she observed, not for the first time. Ed emerged from the office and joined us.

"I heard you say Red Robin. That's a great idea!"

"There are lots of leftovers," my mom tried to sway him. "Don't you think we should have those?"

"No, I'm too tired to cook and clean. Let's go out," Ed said. An alarm sounded in my head, prompting me to lash out at him.

"You said you would fold laundry!"

"I'll do it when we get back from the restaurant," he promised.

"Let's enlist the kids," my mom tried to help. "We

can have a laundry party and watch a movie!" Ignoring her suggestion, I bored my eyes into Ed's.

"When we get back, *you're* going to fold all the laundry and put it away." I marched out.

AFTER DINNER AT THE RESTAURANT, I tried to confide in my mom once more as she helped me get the kids ready for bed.

"I think I need some time off work."

"You have a two-week vacation to Hawaii coming up."

"I'm talking about more than a two-week vacation. Since I didn't take the full recovery time I was entitled to after my knee surgery, I might look into finishing it."

"Do you get paid when you're off for something like that?"

"Yes, I'd get disability."

"How can you afford to live on disability? You have two BMW payments! No one needs two BMWs." I'd expected this conversation while they visited, but I wished it wasn't now.

"We can afford the payments, Mother."

"What about paying back the money you owe me?" she challenged. "Will you be able to afford that, too, on disability?"

Stung, I demanded, "Don't you care more about my health than money?"

"I'm just being practical! You can't take time off if you can't afford it. You should have thought of *that* before you bought a second BMW!" I pressed my lips together and tucked in the kids.

WHEN WE RETURNED to the family room, my stepdad greeted us.

"Ed was just telling me about a movie we should watch," he turned to Ed. "Tell Shelley what it was."

"I didn't mean tonight," Ed headed him off. "I'm too tired to watch a movie."

"You aren't too tired to fold laundry, though," I insisted.

"Ed had to work all day," my mom cut in, again trying to help. "He should go to bed." My mouth fell open.

"I'm going to the kitchen if we're not watching a movie!" Matt stomped out as Ed hugged my mom.

"Thanks, Mom," he said. "I'm going to start Matt's PC first thing tomorrow."

"Oh, good," she encouraged. "Get some rest so you can do that."

"I don't want to do laundry," Juliet, who rarely spoke, complained. My mom overruled her sister.

"You sit there and fold, Juliet! Shelley, you sit down and rest while we take care of this chore," she patted a space beside her on the couch. I wanted to follow Ed to bed, but it was easier to obey. After a short silence, my mom spoke again.

"You don't want to hear this, but I went into your garage yesterday. It's hazardous." She was right. I absolutely did not want to talk about it.

"I know," I opened my work email on my phone.

"Someone is going to trip like you did."

"I didn't trip! I missed the steps going down into the garage," I re-explained the peculiar accident that led to my knee surgery. "Maybe we can find time this weekend to clean it."

"Ed can't do it this weekend. He's fixing Matt's PC," she trapped me in a catch-22.

"Fine! Which do you want? The garage to be safe or Matt's PC to be done?" She didn't answer. I returned to my phone. Dozens of unopened emails in my inbox screamed for attention. I fantasized about deleting every last one.

"I was hoping you'd sit here and visit while we fold laundry," my mom said after a few minutes. "Not play with your phone!"

"I'm not playing with my phone! I'm checking work email."

A moment later, as she retrieved another basket of laundry from the office, my mom stumbled over the same computer case that tripped me earlier in the day. I jumped up to steady her.

"Mom! Are you okay?" She radiated outrage.

"You need to make Ed clean up the office!"

"I'm sorry, I know it's bad. He's going to clean it while we're at Eddie's tournament."

"I thought we were all going on the road trip?" This was my first mention of Ed's staying home.

"Ed has to stay home to work," I explained as I placed the full basket near her seat on the couch, praying she would stop asking questions. I thought my prayer was answered for a few minutes, but I was wrong.

"What are you going to do if the office isn't clean when we get back?" she inquired.

"What do you mean?"

"I mean, how are you going to make him clean it up? You have to *make him* do it," her vehemence took my breath away.

"Or what?"

"You can't let this go any longer," she blew up. "You have to *make him* clean up the office. You have to *make him* clean up the garage!"

"What are you suggesting, Mom?" I demanded aggressively. She stared at me, wobbling on her feet. "Tell me! What do you want me to do? Divorce him because he doesn't keep the garage clean?"

"Well," she said as if it were a complete rebuttal.

"You want me to throw my marriage away because my husband is messy?"

"I don't know what you're going to do, Michelle. All I know is that you used to hate your house being a mess, and now you put up with it. You can't be happy!"

"You let Pop keep your garage a mess! Are you happy with it? Are you going to divorce him because he doesn't keep it neat?"

"No, of course not!"

"Then drop it. I'm going to bed. Good night," I hugged her even though I didn't want to. She was stiff in my arms. "I love you," I offered.

"I love you, too," she replied. When I pulled away, she couldn't resist adding, "I just want to see you happy. I know if your house is like this, you can't be happy!"

I pressed my lips together and marched to the bedroom, straight to the side of the bed where Ed slept.

"Wake up!" I shook his shoulder. "Wake up and listen to me!"

"What's wrong?"

"My mom just tripped and almost fell in the office because of your mess!" I accused.

"What was she doing in the office?"

"Getting a basket of laundry to fold," I said pointedly.

"I told you, I'm going to clean up while you're gone."

"That office better be clean when we get back from the tournament, or—" he trailed off to sleep in front of my eyes. I shook him again. "Wake up!"

"I can't. Too tired…" he snored.

CHAPTER 7

*L*ate Sunday night, I stared down a dozen pharmacy bottles lining the bathroom counter while Ed read in bed. A soft knock sounded on the bedroom door, galvanizing me. I tossed my treasures into a giant Ziplock bag and yelled, "I'll be there in a minute!"

"What's up, Mom?" I overheard Ed.

"I know we were busy all weekend," she answered, "and it was nice for the family to spend time together. But I'm worried about you running out of time to fix Matt's PC."

"Don't sweat it, I've got my time all planned out while you're at Eddie's tournament."

"You're really busy with work. Are you sure you're going to get to it?" I pressed my lips together, zipped the bag, and went to run interference.

"It'll get done, don't worry," Ed was patting her shoulder. "Good night!" I switched places with him.

"Do you need me?" I asked her.

"Yes. Are you taking tomorrow afternoon off, since you had to work when you were supposed to be on vacation?"

"I don't know. I have to see where we're at with the acquisition when I get in." I hadn't told anyone I was planning to take the afternoon off with the intent to see our family doctor.

"You promised you'd teach me how to use Facebook and my bank website. When are we going to do that?"

"We can do that when we're at Eddie's tournament."

"What if there's no internet service? What if we run out of time?" she worried aloud. I lost my patience.

"Mom, quit nagging! No one is forgetting or ignoring you," her back stiffened at my effrontery.

"If I could do these things myself, I would, but I can't. I need your help!" I pressed my lips together and reached out to hug her. We exchanged goodnights. I shut the bedroom door.

"You have to get Matt's PC done," I emphasized to Ed.

"Yes, I know."

"*Before* the final night of their visit!"

"Trust me, I don't want to pull an all-nighter like last time! I'm not in college anymore," he joked.

"It's not funny."

"Oh, come on! It's a little funny. I got it done in time." I pressed my lips together again. The bulging bag of pills was waiting. All weekend I'd deliberated how I'd carry out my plan to quit. I padded to the bathroom and returned, bag dangling from my fist.

"I found a lot of old prescriptions in the bathroom.

I'm going to drop them off at the pharmacy for destruction tomorrow." Ed kept reading. "Did you hear me?"

"What?"

"Never mind."

Down the hall, I pulled the chain for the linen closet light. Pinching a corner of the bag, I aimed and threw it almost to the ceiling. It arced above the tower of quilts on the highest shelf before falling out of sight behind them. To retrieve it would require a ladder we kept in the garage.

AT WORK THE NEXT MORNING, I transferred a half-dozen bottles from my desk drawer into my purse before trudging to the handicapped bathroom, where I could lock the door and be assured of solitude. Clutching the last bottle, I hesitated. What if they clogged the toilet? What if my knee started to hurt? What if I couldn't convince any doctors to give me more? I shook my head and stared at the white ovals sinking in the porcelain bowl. Someone flushed in the bathroom on the other side of the wall. The water jiggled, and they collapsed into a waterlogged mound of powder. Without lifting my eyes, I pushed the lever.

BACK AT MY DESK, I found Monica writing on a sticky note.

"Hello!" she beamed. "I'm happy you're here. Jay scheduled a debrief at two."

"I can't attend. I'm sorry. I have to leave at noon for a doctor's appointment."

"Okay," her resentment seared me like a hot desert wind, but her tone was even. "See if Troy can cover for us." Troy had been tapped to cross-train as back up upon my return from the wedding in Denver. When Monica disappeared into her office, my hand disappeared into the desk drawer. I forgot it was an empty casket. The phone rang.

"Mrs. Black, this is your orthopedic surgeon's office. We received a referral from the ER for persistent postoperative pain."

"Yes?"

"We have an opening tomorrow if you can make it." After agreeing to the appointment, I dashed off a quick email to Monica informing her I'd work from home all day Tuesday. Then, I called to enlist Troy's help.

"Michelle!" he exclaimed. "Are you okay? We heard you were in the hospital."

"Yeah, I passed out on BART."

"Oh, no! What did the doctor say?"

"He referred me to a bunch of specialists. New symptoms crop up all the time," I prepared to launch into a full retelling. "The dizzy spells are getting scary, and—" Troy thwarted me before I could build up steam.

"Hey, Michelle? I only have a minute. How can I help you?" I told him about the upcoming meeting.

"Can you cover for me?"

"I'm swamped," he apologized. "I have to ask Edith if I can push what she asked me to do." Edith was Troy's boss. We all reported to the CFO. Edith had been reluctant to have Troy seconded to me from the get-go, but our entire department was running lean, and Jay had declined to hire an additional analyst.

"Okay, let me know," I hung up and stared out the window at the Transamerica Tower playing peekaboo in the fog. There was a new ache, deep in my right thigh. What if it was a blood clot? What if—the ringing phone stalled my catastrophizing. 'CFO Conference' blinked in the little LED display. I sucked in. It rang twice more. Even after three years of working together, talking to him made me queasy.

"Hi, Jay," I panted.

"Hi, Michelle. Are you in a rush?"

"Sort of. I have to leave soon for an appointment."

"I don't want to make you late. What time do you have to go?"

"Noon," I grudgingly told the truth. It wasn't even 11 o'clock.

"I only need five minutes," he sounded insulted. "Have you recalculated the acquisition analytics since last week?" It was cumbersome to prepare the analysis he wanted to see on an almost-daily basis. Moreover, no matter how many times I ran the model, and no matter how well I knew the numbers, he always questioned my results and recommendations.

"No." He digested my curt answer before replying.

"Okay, we need to recalculate them before this afternoon's meeting. Our CEO is enthusiastic to know how the credit rating agencies view the acquisition, and your analytics are key." A buzzing started in my ears, and the whole world zoomed outward.

"I was in the hospital last week! I have a follow-up this afternoon," panic made my words run together. "There's not enough time for me to run the model before I leave, and I can't miss the appointment!"

"If you can't do it, tell Monica. She'll have to do it."

"Troy is covering for me."

"Edith has Troy working on a project unrelated to the acquisition."

"Monica said Troy could—"

"Troy is not the expert! I don't want him running the model. It's either you, or it's Monica. Let me know who I should expect the analytics from." He hung up. I ran for the bathroom and slammed the door, hyperventilating. It took a half-hour to regulate my breathing.

BACK AT MY DESK, I read an email from Monica, acknowledging my Tuesday plan to work from home. Instead of visiting her to relay the conversation with Jay, I hit reply. It took all the time I had left to perfect my message. Once I sent it, I collected my belongings and waited for the coast to clear before speed-walking to the elevator.

Safely on the train, I breathed a sigh of relief. Eighteen hours had passed since my last OxyContin. My body didn't hurt, but I missed the fuzziness in my head. Everything felt too sharp, too close to me. There was no space between me and my aggravations, as there had been when I floated in an opioid haze. My mom called.

"Are you coming home soon?"

"I'm on BART, headed to see Dr. Drexler."

"You didn't tell me you had an appointment today. Why are you going to Dr. Drexler?" I mentally facepalmed myself.

"She asked me to check in six months after surgery," I lied. The other line beeped. "I have to go, Monica's calling." I swapped over and greeted my boss.

"Michelle, I read your email," I was unsurprised at the frost curling around her words. "It's disappointing that we don't have fresh analytics to share at the meeting."

"I'm sorry, there wasn't time!"

Monica was silent for a moment, then said, "I'll ask Troy to run the model." I cringed, knowing I should tell her about Jay's injunction against Troy working on this project. We said goodbye.

Counting stops as the train doors opened and shut, I began to regret my anxious impulse to schedule this appointment. Dr. Drexler and I had forged a friendship over the years, sharing details of our marriages and kids beyond the usual, dry, doctor-patient conversation. I desperately wanted to unburden my worries, but I feared her powers of perception. What if she saw through my lies? I stared out the window, chewing my right thumb. The raw patch comprised half the area between the nail bed and the first knuckle. I tore at it with my incisors, trying to make it even bigger. When there was one stop left, I dialed.

"I need to cancel an appointment," I sighed with equal parts relief and resignation. A suddenly-free afternoon presented itself.

AN HOUR LATER, my phone rang.

"Hello?" I panted, struggling into a swimsuit in a Macy's changing room.

"Michelle? This is Violet at Dr. Drexler's office. She asked me to give you a call to make sure everything's okay." I stared at myself in the full-length mirror, abundant flesh spilling out in all the wrong places.

"Everything's fine."

"Dr. Drexler is concerned and wants to see you." My instincts had proven correct. Dr. Drexler was no dummy.

"I don't need to see her. I just fainted from standing in a crowded train car in the heat."

"She asked me to reschedule," Vi pressed. It was easier to agree than argue further. We settled on time the following week, and I returned to my image in the mirror. None of the suits were flattering, but this, the largest size ever, was the least ill-fitting. I sat on the changing room bench and stared at my feet, unaware of time passing, eyes going in and out of focus.

Sometime later, I pushed a basket full of clothes I didn't need or remember selecting to the register. I handed the cashier a credit card and was shocked when she said, "Your card was declined, but I'll try again. Sometimes this machine acts up." She handed it back to me after the register squawked a second denial. "I'm sorry. Do you have another form of payment?" Chest tight, I handed over an American Express with no limit.

My mom called as I loaded the car.

"Is your appointment done yet, honey?"

"I'm waiting for a blood draw," I lied. I'd have to hide the shopping bags until I could sneak them past her. I stopped at Target, where I loaded a basket with travel toiletries and LEGO sets for the kids. Approaching the register, my chest tightened again, pins prickling in my shoulder. I held my breath until the card was accepted.

AT HOME, Ed greeted me in the entry.

"Where've you been? I think your mom was expecting you a while ago."

"After Dr. Drexler, I picked up some things we need for Hawaii. Where is everybody?"

"I didn't know you were at the doctor. Your mom walked with the kids to the grocery store. Matt and Juliet are watching TV while I work. You done for the day?"

"No, I need to log on and figure out why Monica hasn't called. Help me get the bags from the car," I beckoned him to follow me. "The Platinum MasterCard got declined at the store, and I have no idea why. It's not near the limit."

"I had to charge some things on it for work," he said.

"How much?"

"About a thousand bucks?" he guessed. The fear

and embarrassment I felt at the registers reared out of nowhere. It felt like a loop of low voltage wire wrapped around my heart.

"Why didn't you use your corporate card?"

"It can't be used for equipment, which is what I bought." I pressed my lips together and locked the car. My mom and the kids rounded the corner onto our street.

"Hurry, let's get this inside," I urged. After we crammed the bags in my side of the closet, I confronted him. "If you use our personal cards for work, you have to tell me. We're in a cash flow nightmare. Our minimum payment's going to be more than we can afford this month now."

"We'll have the reimbursement check in two weeks."

"The payment is due in a couple of days! There's a huge late fee, and the interest rate goes up if we're late again. You'd know that if you paid attention to our finances like I asked you to." For months I'd begged, enlisting his help to right a sinking ship.

"After your mom leaves, we can set aside a night to sit down and go over things. Send me a calendar invite." The wire expanded to encircle my rib cage. I didn't see how this would be any different than the half-dozen times we'd verbally agreed and failed to sit down.

"You seriously want me to email you?"

"Shell, with our crazy schedules, it's the best way to ensure it gets done," he asserted before walking out. I took three steps toward the bathroom before I remembered I'd hidden my pills. It was too late to retrieve them; everyone was milling around, calling out greetings and questions.

WITH THE FAMILY crowded around the kitchen table at dinnertime, my phone vibrated. I excused myself and closed the office door behind me.

"Hello, Monica."

"Do you have a few minutes?"

"We're eating dinner," my tone was only a degree below 'whiny teenager.'

"Well, I'll make this quick because *I* want to get out of the office, too," there was acid in her voice. "We were in Jay's debrief meeting for four hours!"

"You're joking."

"No, I'm not. I asked Troy to recalculate the analytics. He was in a time crunch because of Edith's project," I cringed, making a mental note to put in a thank-you call to Troy. "He hadn't finished at a quarter to, so I decided to go back to the version you prepared last week."

"I'm glad we had it to fall back on," I tried to ease my guilty conscience.

"Unfortunately," she continued, "Troy was editing your presentation. When I printed it, I didn't think to revert to the saved version. You can imagine what happened when Jay saw the numbers." I groaned. A change in the analytics over the week wouldn't be significant, but it would be more than a rounding error. Even if it *were* a rounding error, Jay would have spotted the discrepancy and been on it like a hound on a scent. "Jay spent an hour trying to recreate the numbers before he called Troy. Troy walked us through his calculations, and we discovered a mistake." I clutched my chest to slow my racing heart, squeezing so hard my ribs cracked.

"What did Jay say?" I whispered.

"There was a lot of consternation. The long and short of it is that Jay wants you to run the model and distribute the analytics to the full acquisition team daily going forward."

"I can't do that every day, Monica, it's a huge process! Especially during quarter-end, it'll be impossible! Please, I need a full-time analyst. I've been saying so for eight months!" My seesawing emotions teetered, so close to being out of control.

"I know it's a lot to ask, but Jay doesn't support a new hire for our department right now."

"Can the intern help?"

"She's at capacity. Please send the analysis to the acquisition team every day, starting tomorrow."

After we disconnected, I banged my forehead on the desk until raised voices in the kitchen prompted me to investigate. Ed was nowhere in sight.

"What's going on?" I asked.

"Ed's not going to work on Matt's PC tonight!" my mom wailed.

"Where did he go?"

"He *said* he was going to the bathroom."

"Denise," my stepdad, whose discomfort was

tangible, spoke up. "Ed told you he'd do it while we're at the tournament, so quit bugging Shelley."

"Matt, someone has to *make him* do what he promised," my mom reverted to her mantra from laundry night.

Eddie's fierce protective instinct kicked in, and he said, "My daddy always does what he promises!"

"Eddie," I admonished, trying to short circuit a family argument, "do not talk to your grandmother that way! Apologize this instant." I caught his injured look, but he complied.

"Sorry, Grams."

"Mom," I turned to her and spoke forcefully. "We are not rehashing this at the dinner table!"

"I'm not saying anything that isn't true," she persisted.

"We're not doing this. Speak with Ed directly." I was exhausted, and the call with Monica had stolen my appetite. "Eddie and Elsie, clear the table and get ready for bed." They obeyed. My mom and I washed dishes, bouncing off each other's chill silence. When we retired to the living room, I felt as though I'd run a marathon.

Eddie appeared in pajamas and wet hair.

"Mom! Elsie and I are ready for bed. Will you tuck us in?" I was too tired to stand, so I passed the buck to my mom.

"Grams will."

"We want you."

"Mommy," Elsie called from the hallway. "We want you!"

"Fine," my mom harrumphed. "You don't want

Grams? See if I take you to the park again while I'm here!" I remembered the way her mother used the same emotional blackmail on me as a child. It worked like a charm. Elsie came running to shed tears of apology in my mom's lap while Eddie backpedaled.

"Grams, I'm sorry! You can come, too. We like it when you take us to the park." I pressed my lips together and lumbered to my feet.

When I tucked Eddie in, he whispered a question.

"Mom, why does Grams say bad stuff about Dad? I don't like it!"

I tried to explain, saying, "Your grandmother is just worried that Daddy's too busy to finish the favor he promised to do for her. It's happened before." His forehead crinkled up, but he didn't say anything else.

I kissed Elsie goodnight in the next room, then stared longingly at the linen closet door. I pressed my lips together and shuffled back to the family room where my mom had rejoined Matt and Juliet. Too weary to uphold my end of the argument, I apologized.

"Mom, I'm sorry I spoke to you that way at dinner, but you can't criticize Ed in front of the kids. I'm not okay with it."

"Well, I'm not okay with Ed not fixing Matt's PC," she rejoined.

"Are we going to watch a movie tonight or not?" Matt interjected.

I seized on the change of subject, saying, "How about *The Fifth Element*?"

"You made us watch that before," my mom sounded resentful and unwilling to forgive yet. "I don't like action movies, and I don't like watching the same movie twice!" She similarly shot down the rest of my movie suggestions until Ed joined us. "There you are," she pinned him. "I figured you went to bed!"

"I told you I was going to the bathroom," he said testily. "My stomach is bothering me. I think it's the leftovers."

"No one else has an upset stomach," she pointed out. "Have you seen a doctor? Your stomach bothers you an awful lot for a healthy man your age." Desperate to avoid more conflict over leftovers, I tried to redirect the conversation.

"What movie should we watch?"

"Have you seen *Butch Cassidy and the Sundance Kid*?" Matt asked.

"Yes, Matt," my mom answered tartly. "We've all seen it. Several times! No one wants to watch a Western."

"I'm trying to help!" his feelings were wounded.

"Think of something from this century to watch, then," she instructed. I felt pins and needles all over my body, and my heart beat in its new, unsteady gallop. This may as well have been another recurring nightmare.

"We're going to watch *Rush Hour*," Ed settled the question.

An hour into the movie, everyone but me was snoring. I deserted them and settled in bed, the wall next to my head shaking with explosions at the climax of the movie. Lydia was floating on the edge of my mind. I picked up the ragged memory where I'd recently left off.

∞

"Do you want to get a room upstairs?" she whispered in my ear as we sat on the red couch. I twisted to face her.

"Upstairs? Now?"

"Yeah, why not? It *is* a hotel, and I told Bill I'd be out late." I didn't want to say no, but I wasn't ready to say yes. I stalled by posing some of the questions I'd filed away.

"How many girlfriends have you had? Does Bill know about them all?" Lydia was far ahead of me in same-sex explorations. Among my friend group, polyamory was unknown. Bisexuality and swinging were joked about but not practiced.

"I've had a few," she hedged. "Actually, Bill knew before I did that I was bisexual. He helped me see it and encouraged me to explore. Bill has my permission to have a girlfriend, but he hasn't taken advantage of it yet." I was intrigued. I'd never considered Ed's having a girlfriend, only me.

"Does Bill get jealous?"

"Sometimes, but he knows I can't live without a woman's touch." She thought a moment before clarifying, "He's my soulmate, but there's a hole in our relationship he can't fill." Her description of their relationship made me ache inside.

"You said Bill would have to meet me before we could be intimate," I reminded her.

"I don't always play by the rules," she smiled devilishly. "Bill can meet you later. Right now, I want you." We'd arrived at the point where my bravado outweighed my commitment.

"Ed expects me for dinner."

"You haven't even finished your wine!" Lydia's fiery reaction startled me. "You're trying to escape. I knew you were too good to be true!"

"I told Ed I was only auditioning you tonight, and I need him to trust me if this is going to work," I explained. As far as Ed knew, I was having drinks with coworkers.

"I want to be your first!"

"I haven't liked anyone else well enough even to meet face-to-face," I lied with a coquettish grin. "You're the only one I'm interested in." Lydia blushed.

"When can we get together again?"

"Ed goes on a business trip in a couple of weeks. I could meet Bill, and perhaps you and I could go on a date while he's gone?" She seemed satisfied.

When we exited the hotel lobby, she grabbed my arm and pulled me into a dark corner of the portico. Our untoned mom-tummies squished against each other in the tight space. I smelled the sour dregs of wine on her mouth as she inclined her head to mine. I loved being chased, playing matador. But only to a point. My discomfort spiked fast.

"You're a good kisser!" I purred, breaking free from her grasp.

"You're teasing me, aren't you?" she groaned, emerging from the cubbyhole after me. I didn't reply. We walked next to each other, my right pinky brushing her left one, as she tried to hook our hands together. I deftly kept my fingers free. At my car door, I turned to face her.

"Thanks for meeting me. I'll message you later?" She leaned in for another kiss, but I gave her my cheek. "Good night," I was firm.

"Good night, babydoll." I hated that she'd already taken to calling me pet names.

I TUCKED THE MEMORY AWAY. My body was still. Instead of turned on, I felt sad. Ed opened the bedroom door in the darkness. I hadn't noticed the TV go silent. I played opossum and must have fallen asleep before he climbed in bed because the next thing I knew, it was Tuesday morning.

CHAPTER 8

*T*uesday afternoon, I was deep in thought working on the inaugural daily distribution of the acquisition analytics, as ordered by Jay. Grandparents and kids traipsed in and out of the house, swimming and eating and playing. Ed wore noise-canceling headphones at his desk. My mom cracked the door after I ignored the ringing landline.

"Shell? There's a call from your orthopedic surgeon's office."

"Mom, why did you pick up?" I whined. "I don't want to talk to them!"

"Well, I'm sorry I didn't know," she said, defensive. "The phone rang, and I answered it like you're supposed to!" I pressed my lips together and picked my way across the field of detritus to take the call in the kitchen.

"Mrs. Black, I'm calling about the appointment you missed today," I recognized the voice of the same scheduler who'd called me at work the day prior. "We have a cancellation at 4:30. We'll waive the missed appointment fee if you can make it." I wondered when they began enforcing the rules about missed appointments. If I'd known, I would've thought twice about skipping it.

"I'm sorry I can't make it. Is there any chance you can waive the fee?" I felt her frustration. This wasn't the first time she'd dealt with my bait-and-switch.

"Just this time, we can make an allowance," she sighed. "Do you want to reschedule?"

"No, thanks." My mom barely waited for me to hang up.

"Did you forget an appointment today?"

"Yes."

"Did they waive the fee?"

"Yes!" I was impatient to get back to work.

"What did Dr. Drexler say yesterday? You never told me." I sighed in the back of my throat.

"She was pleased with my progress and encouraged me to keep up physical therapy." I hoped this sort-of-true answer—I still went like clockwork, twice a week, for rehabilitation—would be enough to ward off further questioning.

"What did she say about the fact that your knee still hurts sometimes? Like when you tripped at the party," my mom asked, following me back to the office.

"Nothing, Mom," I started to worry about her intuition. "It's normal."

"I talked to Mary about your surgery," she referred to a long-time family friend. "Mary's a nurse practitioner, you know, so she has medical training. She told me that taking painkillers for more than six months in a row is dangerous."

"Do I look like an addict?" I rounded on her, suddenly hostile. "Am I staying in bed and skipping work and scrabbling for pills?"

"No, of course not," she looked surprised. "What I'm trying to tell you is, Mary's daughter Bernie—" I didn't allow her to finish.

"I am *not* an addict!" I yelled. Mary's daughter, Bernice, was two years older than me. Since we were teenagers, Bernice had fought addiction. Mary was forever bailing her out. I was terrified of being compared to her.

"I know you're not, Michelle! If you'd let me finish, I'm not talking about Bernie's *problem*," she emphasized 'problem' the same way she'd said I 'used' medications. "Bernie had a surgery that went wrong. She didn't realize it for the longest time because the doctor kept prescribing painkillers and saying the pain was normal. She had to have two more surgeries to fix it! *That's* what I'm worried about."

"That's not going to happen to me," I dismissed her concern, relieved she didn't suspect me.

"How do you know?"

"Mom, my procedure was a success. All my check-ups have been great."

"Then why are you still in pain sometimes?" she worried aloud. I pressed my lips together and recalled her reaction to my idea of taking disability leave. "I want to know if you're having trouble. I want to help! We live so far away from each other. This kind of thing wouldn't happen if you lived closer to me." Unexpected panic overwhelmed me.

"We're not moving to Arizona, ever. I hate Arizona! I left there for a reason. I have to get back to work!" I couldn't stop the memory that reared out of nowhere.

∞

I WAS in PE class in fifth grade. I raced up the gridiron, football tucked neatly under my arm, red flags at my waist snapping in the desert breeze. I couldn't believe I caught a pass! Behind me, my teammates cheered.

"Shelley! Wait!" The PE coach's words reached me too late. I crossed into the end zone and turned to do a victory dance. One of the boys on the other team caught up. He yanked my flags and ran circles around me.

"Rusty! Give it back now!" I was furious at his interference. Everyone caught up as Rusty laughed and flicked the belt out of reach over my head.

"Shelley, you ran the ball into your team's end zone," Coach panted.

"That's a touchdown, right?" I asked. The boys groaned. Bethany, my sole female teammate, rolled her eyes and turned to Coach.

"She scored against us, didn't she?"

"Yes," Coach said. "That's a safety for Rusty's team." I couldn't believe it.

"But I caught the ball and ran all the way from the other end of the field!"

"Shelley, this is *your* team's end zone," Coach corrected me. "You want to carry the ball into the *other* team's end zone to earn a touchdown." My face was hot with embarrassment and the effort of my long sprint. Bethany waited till Coach was out of earshot.

"You're an idiot!" she sneered. "I don't want you on my team." After the next play, I told Coach my stomach hurt and sat out the remainder of the game.

"Mom!" I yelled, slamming open the door at home after I got off the bus. My chest was splitting with unshed tears.

"I'm right here," she was in the kitchen, looking at papers strewn across the tabletop. I stopped short.

"What are those?"

"Divorce papers. I'm trying to figure out how I'm going to make things work!" I felt her deep distress.

"What do you mean?"

"I mean, I have to figure out how to support us."

"Do we have to move?"

"Yes! This house is too big. We're going to have to take in boarders to help with expenses until I get on my feet and start a job." Taking in boarders sounded like something they did back in the *Little House on the Prairie* days to me.

"What are you going to do?" I was worried about having to share one of my bedrooms.

"This may surprise you, but I have an education," she reacted with wounded pride. "I was planning to work until your dad decided I would stay home. I'll have to go back and finish my degree." It sounded very grown-up and official. She started crying. "I don't understand why your dad doesn't want me anymore! How could he do this to me? To us!" Her watery blue eyes searched mine. Unsure what she expected, I tried to be mature beyond my eleven years.

"Mom, don't cry. It's going to be okay!" Her trickle of tears gushed into a waterfall.

"I did everything he wanted! I took care of you, and I even sold cosmetics door-to-door to help with household expenses. He never had to ask anything from me. Why is this happening?"

"We're going to be okay, Mom, I promise. I can sell some of my toys!"

"Don't be ridiculous, Shelley," she rejected my childish offer, blew her nose on a crinkled tissue, and tried to smile. "How was school today?"

"My team won our flag football game in PE," I lied cheerfully. "I scored a touchdown!"

THE YELLOW KITCHEN of my childhood dissolved, but I was still face-to-face with my mom, who was crying.

"If I'm such a burden and I nag so much, then I guess we'll go home and quit bothering you!"

"That's not what I meant," I could barely speak over the decades-old lump in my throat.

"How would I know that? You act like you don't want me here! You promise to take a vacation when we come, and then you work the whole time. I try to help around the house, but you contradict every decision I make." I pressed my lips together and let her fume. "You're my only daughter, and I'm not going to live forever. We should be spending time now as a family! I would give anything to have more time with my mom and dad now that they're gone." It was easier to apologize than explain my feelings.

"I'm sorry. We can spend a lot of mother-daughter time together on the road trip," I offered what I didn't want to give.

"Okay, I'd like that," she blew her nose on the ever-present crinkled tissue. We hugged, détente achieved for the moment.

BACK AT MY DESK, I had to re-login. A flurry of new emails had settled in my inbox. They all shared the same subject: *CEO & Board Meeting NEXT WEEK*. Panic rose so fast that I pushed my desk chair back and swung my head between my knees for fear I might faint.

When the miasma lifted, I was astonished to find myself standing in the bathroom, two Xanax nestled in my palm. I shrugged and told myself, "*If I can just make it to Hawaii, everything is going to be okay.*" Down went the pills. No sooner than the cold water accompanying them hit my stomach, I panicked all over again. What if taking two was too much? What if I started slurring, and someone guessed what I'd done? I shook my head. I didn't have a choice. I marched back to the office, where an urgent email from Monica lurked.

"I know you're on vacation for the remainder of the week," it read, "but we may need you. We'll minimize interruptions. Troy will cover meetings while you're out. Please coordinate with him before you take off."

"Got it. Will do," I hit send, then started making a list. I only got as far as 'pack suitcases' and 'collect Eddie's gear' when Troy called.

"I saw Monica's email. Can we please talk before you're out of the office?" he asked. I felt the day slipping away and the pressure of an early-morning departure.

"I can't do that until I send the daily analytics email." I knew it was ungracious, but I couldn't resist adding, "And I have personal business to attend to so I can't work late."

"I don't want to work late, either, especially since the next week is beginning to look like a massive fire drill!" My empath sense kicked in belatedly, reminding me that it was unfair to expect him to know this job yet. I relented.

"I know. I'm sorry. We'll spend as much time as you need after I send the email."

I tried to refocus on my task. I fiddled with the model, growing frustrated by the mushy state of my brain. I thought I'd finalized it in the morning, but I was now convinced it contained errors. I made change after change, striking the keyboard and mouse in a staccato symphony of indecision. I printed paper copies of data and checked numbers once, twice, three times. I switched to email. Drafting took little time, but I got sidetracked while editing. I wrote and rewrote sentences, punctuated one way and back again, then opened the thesaurus and started replacing words. Before I knew it, it was late afternoon.

"ETA for the email?" Monica messaged me on the internal chat app.

"I thought I had till EOD," I typed back forcefully.

"We should get ahead of it," she replied. Instead of finishing the email, I called Troy, who was ready to go with a list of questions.

"Why is our credit rating so important to us?"

"For a couple of reasons…" I found the rhythm of teaching despite the black magic of the Xanax. We talked at length until little bubbles popped up in the chat window, still open on my conversation with Monica. I stared at them while Troy finished what he'd been saying.

"We proved through the recession that we have a strong business, right?" he asked.

"That's true."

"Then why is Jay so worried about how this one small acquisition will affect it?" My chat app beeped, and I saw that Monica had only sent, 'ETA?' Smashing down worry that something was amiss with the email or the model, I hit send before answering Troy.

"He's worried because The Westing Group changed our rating outlook from 'stable' to 'negative' a few months back." Westing was one of the larger agencies that rated our company. "Do you remember?"

"I could do with a refresher."

"Well, Westing was not a fan of some strategic moves we made early in the year. By putting us on a 'negative' outlook, it means they're watching for more decisions they disagree with. If there are enough of those within 18 months, they'll downgrade us. A downgrade will significantly drive up our cost of doing business, so Jay doesn't want to give them any reason to downgrade."

"Nothing bad came from those decisions, so why haven't they changed the outlook back to 'stable'?" I had devoted many hours to answering this very question. I repeated my findings to Troy.

"Remember 2008? It seemed like the economy would grow forever. Everyone was buying second and third homes. Banks were offering risky mortgages to win market share."

"I remember all of that," he confirmed. "I was a bond trader back then. There were so many mortgage bonds to choose from! Everything was rated AAA."

"Exactly. The banks were putting all those mortgages they made in bonds, then selling them to investors. The credit rating agencies were supposed to assess the riskiness of the bonds. Like everyone else, they got lulled into thinking the real estate market would never go down. This was fine as long as the economy was going strong. The problem was, when the economy stumbled, they kept assigning high ratings to mortgage bonds, thinking real estate was invulnerable."

"Everybody drank everybody else's Kool-Aid!" Troy gave a wry half-laugh, signifying he understood.

"Well, after the recession ended, regulators determined that the credit rating agencies were too slow to downgrade the mortgage bonds at the root of the problem. As a result, they got a big portion of the blame for the market collapse."

"I remember the huge government fines and new regulations."

"Yes. You might be wondering how all this answers your question about why The Westing Group hasn't returned our outlook to 'stable.'"

"I barely remembered that was where we started!" Troy teased.

"Funny," I acknowledged. "The credit rating agencies don't want to be blamed for another recession, so they overhauled all of their rating processes. They put rules in place to safeguard their independence and enforce ethical behavior. We're one of the first companies to be judged by the new rules."

"...and one of Westing's new rules is to keep a 'negative' outlook for eighteen months. That way, nothing surprises them once they establish a cause for concern," Troy finished the lesson on my behalf.

"Yes, see? You understand perfectly," I congratulated him. Mastery achieved, Troy wished me safe travels. I logged off, relieved to be done with my workday. Before the screen wiped, a notification appeared. I glimpsed that it was from Jay. Adrenaline jolted through me.

"No, no, no...please don't let there be a mistake..." I chanted, heart racing in an instant.

"What's up?" Ed asked from his seat behind me.

"I finally got that stupid email sent, and as I was signing off, Jay replied to it!"

"You're officially on vacation. Jay can get what he needs from Monica." I ignored him, racing to type my password correctly as my skin crawled from head to toe. I opened Jay's email, and my stomach dropped.

"Michelle, where is the model? I asked you to include it." He'd copied everyone. A chat message appeared from Troy.

"Jay needs the model." As if on cue, more pop-ups appeared, all bearing some version of the same message. They spawned like porn ads. My cell rang.

"Yes, Monica, I know! I'm trying to get the model attached and sent."

"As long as you're aware of the situation."

"Yes, thank you, goodbye."

"Why don't I stay on the line until you send it? I can confirm it was received."

"Sure," I growled through bared teeth. Monica waited while I found the latest iteration of the model, dodging chat notifications the whole time. "I'm sending it now."

"Great," Monica went silent, but I could hear her mouse clicking in the background. "Got it. Have a good trip!"

Mistake amended, I lurched to my feet. A sheen of nervous sweat clung to me, and my heart pounded against the inside of my ribs. I cursed myself for putting my pills out of reach in such a central location and made a beeline for the door.

"Did you get it taken care of?" Ed stopped me.

"Yes, but if one more person complains about my forgetting the attachment, I'm going to lose it!"

"Mmmmmm...yeah," he took up the shtick from *Office Space*. "I'm gonna have to go ahead and ask you to redistribute that TPS report. And don't forget the cover sheet this time!" I burst into tears, much to his dismay. "What's wrong?"

"I hate working with the rating agencies! It's not what I want to do!"

"Get a new job. I've been telling you that for years." My mind flashed to Wisconsin, but I couldn't wage that battle again.

"When Monica got me that big raise, it priced me out of the market for similar jobs," I deflected. "I don't have an MBA!"

"You don't need an MBA. Remember Wells Fargo? And LeapFrog? And Dolby?" he ticked down the list of big-name companies in the Bay Area where I'd interviewed over the years. In all three instances, I'd made it to the last two candidates before being passed on. Remembering those lost opportunities was depressing.

"What's the point of getting a different job? I hate working in finance, but I'm stuck."

"The problem isn't finance," Ed dismissed my objection. "It's that no one at work knows how to tell Jay no. It's a toxic environment." While this was true, it was *my* toxic environment. The enemy I knew seemed safer than the one unmet. This was deeper than we'd delved into my recent feelings about work.

"What if no one will hire me?" I asked in a small voice, revealing a secret fear.

"Then do something else!" he exhorted. "Apply for medical school. Start taking night classes to get your prerequisites. It's always been your dream." Harsh reality lurked behind the pretty words.

"How are we going to afford that!" It wasn't a question.

"I don't know, but we'll figure it out. We always figure things out! Everyone knows we make a great team." Now fantasy was the culprit behind the words.

"Ed, we live paycheck to paycheck! We cannot afford for me to quit my job!" My mom knocked on the door and cracked it.

"What's going on in here? Shell, I heard you crying."

"Shell's had a rough afternoon at work," Ed walked over to hug me.

"Oh, my baby! I'm so sorry," my mom came in to wrap her arms around us both. "I'm glad you're finally on vacation."

"I might have to work while we're at the tournament," I sniffled, delivering my news quickly while her sympathy was fresh.

"You can still go on the trip, though?" she hoped.

"Yeah, I can go, I just have no idea when work will spring on me," I cried harder. "I won't be able to relax! I never get downtime anymore!"

"Shh, shh. It's okay," my mom pushed Ed's arms off and took over cuddling me while I cried gut-wrenching sobs. Elsie wandered in to find us in this sad mural.

"Momma? Why are you crying?" I shoved my mom away and stood ramrod straight, wiping tears on the backs of my hands.

"I'm fine, Elsie! Nothing for you to worry about," I

smothered a cry-hiccup. She looked from me to my mom and back again.

"Grams and Aunt Juliet and I are playing Spa Day. Want to get a manicure and a massage?"

"Can I visit your spa later? I need to rest after work."

"Let me get my appointment book," Elsie looked excited. My mom watched her bustle off, then turned to me with tears in her eyes.

"She's going to put you on her schedule! Isn't that adorable?" I couldn't see the cuteness in Elsie's actions, and I didn't want to feel my mom's affectionate delight. It was all too much.

"I have to pack for the trip," I said, ducking out of reach when she tried to pull me back in her embrace.

"You go ahead and do that. I can reheat leftovers for dinner." Her words caught the ear of Ed, who had returned to his desk.

"What leftovers?" he asked, suspicious.

I escaped, pausing to deliberate in the hall between the linen closet and Elsie's bedroom door. The Ziplock bag was only a few feet away from me. I longed for the bliss of four opioid-filled days at Eddie's tournament, untethered from work. I grabbed a thick scar on my right thigh and pinched hard. Despair washed over me and into tide pools hidden in the deep places of my body. Elsie came out of her room roleplaying.

"Hello, ma'am! What Spa Day services are you interested in?" It took every ounce of my self-control to play along.

CHAPTER 9

"*D*enise, I want to get on the road before midnight!" my stepdad prodded. He stood with Ed and me on the driveway, watching my mom kiss and hug the kids, who did not want their Grams to go. She waved him off. "I don't understand these long, drawn-out goodbyes. Watch, here's how we do it in the Midwest," he pulled me in for a brief embrace. "Love ya. Bye!" He then raised his hand in salute to Ed. "Ed, see you soon. We'll look for the computer shipment, so let us know when it's on its way." He slammed the driver's door and revved the engine. Juliet was already buckled in the back seat, having dispensed her hugs early. We'd been home from our road trip for 48 tense hours.

"Mom, seriously," I urged as politely as I could. "I've got to get the kids to camp and myself to work." Guilt washed over me. I wasn't sure our farewell would be pleasant. Not only had I failed to teach her the things she'd asked for my help with while on the road trip, but we'd arrived home to find Ed had not begun work on Matt's PC. I was relieved when she held me tight and whispered in my ear.

"I love you! I miss you so much when I'm not here." She turned to Ed. "You're the best son-in-law ever! Thank you for all the hard work you do, and thank you for taking care of my babies." I pressed my lips together and watched them tearfully hug. Once she made it into the passenger seat, she waved at us until they disappeared around the corner.

Back indoors, Ed's eyes followed me while I readied the kids and collected my briefcase. He tried to talk to me.

"Shell, I can tell you're upset with me for not finishing Matt's computer."

"I'm upset at you for way more than that!" I unleashed my pent-up frustration.

"Yes, I know," he sighed. "I'm sorry I didn't get a start on the office or garage."

"You shouldn't have committed to so much!"

"I expected to have time," he reasoned, "but work was nuts."

"That's no surprise! Work always comes first with you. I felt abandoned on the road trip. Did you even care that you weren't there?" I felt a panic attack lurking.

"Of course, I cared! I missed all of you terribly," he protested. "I'm going to work on the garage next weekend." My shoulders slumped.

"Whatever. I have to get the kids to camp." He turned to walk down the bedroom hall. "Where do you think you're going?" I yelled after him. He turned back to me.

"I need to sleep, Shell. I've been up for 24 hours straight trying to finish Matt's computer. I can't think anymore." The nightmare plane crash feeling took hold.

"Gee, it must be nice to do whatever you want whenever you want!" I sneered before slamming the front door.

In the community center parking lot, Eddie repeated the question he'd asked me at his final game.

"Mom, why didn't Dad come to my tournament?"

"Honey, I told you," I said in a faux-cheerful tone. "Daddy had a lot of work that couldn't wait, so he had to stay home. It was fun anyway, wasn't it? Pop and Grams and Aunt Juliet were there, and Elsie, too! Remember the swim park between games?" Diverted, he and Elsie shared memories of the lazy river until I signed them in. Eddie bounced off to join his group. Elsie hung back.

"Mommy," she admonished. "Daddy had a lot of work to do. You shouldn't be mad at him." I pressed my lips together, wishing I could defend myself but settling for a scolding.

"Remember what Mrs. Waylon used to say? Mind your own business!" I quoted her kindergarten teacher.

On the train to San Francisco, I stared out the window

and worried at my thumb. I wondered what waited for me at work. I'd barely heard a peep while I was out, and Xanax was doing little to ease the building wave of anxiety. Of course, Monica called.

"Good morning," I answered, conscious of my tardiness. "I'm on my way in."

"Heads-up. Jay set a lunchtime call to prep for the meeting with the CEO and Board. You're on the agenda." I shifted attention from my thumb, which had taken on the look of raw hamburger meat, to my index finger.

At the office, a whirlwind of preparation swept me up. Midmorning, I took a break to swallow two more Xanax and a ginormous breakfast burrito. At noon I dialed into the conference and waited my turn.

"Michelle," Jay called, setting my heart pounding. "How do you expect the credit rating agencies to react based on the current forecast?" I knew he wasn't going to like my answer, which I tried to deliver in an unwavering voice.

"Under the new regulations, it doesn't look promising. This acquisition will erode profitability enough to justify at least one, perhaps two, of the credit rating agencies downgrading us."

"Has Monica reviewed your work?" The question felt like an insult.

"Yes, both she and Edith have." I crossed my fingers that he would move to the next person on the agenda.

"What have you done to refute it?" he asked. I drew a blank.

"To refute…what?"

"What have you done to refute The Westing Group's 'negative' outlook on our rating?" An inner alarm sounded. This question was specific and beyond the scope of a check-in, but I couldn't refuse to answer.

"Their negative outlook is based on strategic decisions we made earlier—"

"I'm aware of *why* their outlook is what it is," he cut me off. "What are you *doing* about it?" A smattering of laughter echoed on the line. Heat rose from my toes to my crown, and my voice faltered.

"I—I'm okay with doing whatever you like, Jay, but their outlook will stick for a minimum of eighteen months. I can show you the new rules they published."

"It's *your* job to figure out how we're going to change their mind. Let's take this offline. Call Penny and get on my calendar." He moved on.

Monica came to find me after the call.

"I have a slot with Jay today. I don't need all of it, so you can piggyback on my time."

"Monica, what's he talking about?" I implored. I'd been tearing my hair out, wondering how I was supposed to execute Jay's directive. "We can't refute the methodology! It's a mathematical equation applied to public financial results."

"You'll have to ask Jay," her energy was evasive. In a consolatory voice, she added, "Edith heard in some senior executive sessions that he wants to manage the rating agencies differently than we have in the past." My empath sense twinged vaguely.

. . .

LATER, when I accompanied Monica to the top floor, my concern sharpened. Jay was surprised to see me, and not in a good way.

"Michelle, I told you to call Penny and get on my calendar. Are we meeting now?"

"No, Jay," Monica answered for me. "You and I are meeting now. I don't need the full appointment, so I offered my unused portion to Michelle."

"*You* may not need the whole time with *me*; however, *I* may need the whole time with *you*," Jay said. He turned to his assistant. "Penny, find a different slot for Michelle. What time do I have to leave?" Penny clicked her mouse and peered into her screen.

"You're meeting your wife at 8:00 at Michael Mina. Your only opening is at 5:30."

"Book it," he instructed. To me, he said, "See you later, Michelle." I smiled unctuously, stomach roiling. When Monica and Jay disappeared behind his heavy mahogany door, Penny grimaced.

"Sorry about that, Michelle. He schedules himself too tight. If I gave you any other time, you'd get pushed till then anyway. Better to tell you upfront."

"I can't do this," I uttered.

"What?"

"I can't do this!"

"Do you need a different time? I can try to shuffle some other folks around, but—"

"I have to get out of here!" I flew down the stairs to the mezzanine that adjoined the two executive floors and hammered on the elevator call button. I jumped when the doors parted to reveal our Chief Marketing

Officer inside the lift. My start startled him, which startled me again. Papers spilled from my arms, and my calculator bounced over his feet. A Southern gentleman through and through, Mason collected them and rested his hand on my heaving shoulder.

"Michelle, are you okay? What's troubling you?" I wracked my brain for a cogent reply.

"I don't know what I'm supposed to do about The Westing Group." Mason knew all about the situation with the rating agencies. "Jay is posing questions I can't answer, and asking me to do things I'm not sure I understand. I'm afraid I'm going to do something wrong, say something wrong! What if we get downgraded?" He braced my shoulder.

"You're one smart lady. I bet you know just what to do." I searched his face for a better answer. Nothing was forthcoming. The elevator protested Mason's foothold with a hoarse alarm, too much like the jangling of my nerves. I willed my rampant emotions into stillness. Once suspended, I wadded them into a tight ball that I hid in the space below my diaphragm. I imagined an iron manhole cover clanging down over it.

"Mason, I'm sorry," my voice was silken, giving the lie to my Jekyll/Hyde moment. "Excuse me, I've got to get some things done." Taken aback, he withdrew his hand from my shoulder and his foot from between the doors.

Downstairs at my desk, the unnatural calm continued. When I saw Monica return from Jay's office ten minutes later, I decided to call Ed.

"I need you to get the kids from camp tonight."

"Why?"

"I have a meeting with Jay at 5:30."

"That's after the end of the business day! Why did you agree to that?" My hard-won calm shattered.

"I didn't have a choice! I never have a choice about anything anymore!" The intern poked her head out of her cubicle to see why my voice was raised. I lowered it. "Is there a problem with your getting the kids? Do you already have something else planned?"

"No, that's not the point—" I didn't wait for him to say more.

"Fine. You're getting them from camp. I'll see you when I get home." I hung up.

At 5:30 on the nose, I returned to the executive suite.

"He's on a call," Penny informed me. "He asked if you could come back at six o'clock."

"Can I wait here in case he finishes early?"

"When has Jay ever been done with anything early?" she laughed. I thought about Monica returning to her desk that afternoon and shrugged. Penny nodded toward the waiting area, "Suit yourself."

Six o'clock arrived and passed. At ten after, Penny stuck her head in Jay's office and reminded him I was waiting. I heard his reply.

"Thanks, Penny. You can head home." She shut the door and looked at me.

"He knows you're here."

It wasn't until 6:45 when the waiting area lights had

shut off twice, and I had to wave my arms to re-illuminate them, that he emerged.

"Hey, Michelle, are you ready?"

"I've been ready for over an hour," I remarked, sulkiness leaking into my tone. He gave me a measured gaze before stepping back, and made a point of holding open his office door for me.

"Let's get this done." I pressed my lips together and spread my materials on the conference table. Instead of sitting with me, he perused a few items on his desk, put on his glasses, and sat at his computer with an offhand, "Just a minute, I want to check something."

After five minutes, I thought he'd forgotten me. I coughed gently, to no avail. My phone buzzed.

"On your way home yet?"

"No, waiting on Jay." The delivery notification flipped straight to a read receipt. A minute or two passed. I texted again.

"What are you feeding the kids?" The notification didn't change. Jay kept working.

"I asked a question," I tried to provoke a response. Still, the delivery notification did not flip. Jay's typing picked up the tempo in time with the omnipresent anxious beat inside me. I texted again.

"Answer me!" The beat turned into a cacophony. What if something happened to one of the kids? What if the house caught on fire? The catastrophes in my head multiplied like wildfire. At the turn of seven o'clock, when the manhole cover was on the verge of exploding and ripping through my guts, Jay reanimated.

"Okay, let's get this done," he sat across from me

and folded his hands expectantly. I pointed to the stapled packet in front of him.

"I put together the information about Westing's methodology and a comparison of the key metrics that apply to this acquisition."

"That's not what I need. I know all that." My mind raced. What was I missing? What was he asking for? I finally asked.

"What do you need? I know you're hopeful that The Westing Group will reconsider their negative outlook, but—"

"Romy doesn't know about this acquisition yet, right?" Romy was our analyst at Westing. It was her opinion that had placed us on probation, and in danger of a downgrade that would cause a major dent in our financial results.

"No, she doesn't."

"Then how can you be certain she won't reconsider?" I reframed my argument.

"The new methodology is cut and dried, Jay. Plus, Romy told me her management is inflexible: a negative outlook stands for at least eighteen months. Ours only changed a few months ago. Romy has to follow the rules." He was unmoved.

"I want you to preview this acquisition with Romy. Ask for an informal opinion." I could not see how doing this would cause her to consider our request in a positive light, but I *could* see how it might put her in an awkward position under the new rules. I wanted to say so, but suddenly I questioned my understanding. What if I was wrong? What if Jay saw something I'd missed?

What if—I silenced the what-if game. I didn't have a choice.

"Okay, I'll call Romy tomorrow."

"Let me know as soon as you talk to her." I left him clacking away at his keyboard. On my way to the elevator, I popped a Xanax at the drinking fountain.

CHAPTER 10

*E*arly the next morning, head pounding from too much tequila and a tense evening at home, I prepared to carry out Jay's order. Staring at the phone, I recalled how ill-humored Romy had been lately. In one candid moment, she uncharacteristically complained to me of a company that hounded her for weeks after she wrote an unflattering opinion. They ambushed her with a full panel of C-level executives on a conference call to try to change her mind, and her resentment was fearsome. I buried my distaste before I dialed her number.

"Hi, Romy! How's your summer been?" My voice was too bright.

"Hot and humid," she sounded distracted. "What do you need?"

"Jay asked me to give you a call and beg your insight on a potential acquisition."

"Is this an acquisition you're already pursuing, or is it purely brainstorming?"

"Which do I have to say to get you to help me?" I joked nervously.

Unamused, Romy replied, "Michelle, The Westing Group adopted a new ethics code concerning requests for informal opinions, which I sent to you. I can't talk to you like I did in the old days before the recession. Just like companies are no longer allowed to 'whisper' previews of earnings before they're publicly announced, rating agencies are no longer allowed to give opinions on acquisitions until they're publicly announced."

Desperate to appease Jay, I ignored my misgivings and said, "This is something we're actively looking at."

"I see," she telegraphed wariness. "I did hear rumors that you're considering acquiring a company in an adjacent state."

"That's the one," I confirmed.

"Has Jay even read the note I wrote last spring?" she asked, exasperated. "It says, in plain English, 'further steps that extend the company's business beyond its core strengths could add negative rating pressure.' This acquisition fits that bill perfectly! It is not only a new line of business; it's outside your current geographic footprint. You bet it's going to cause downward rating pressure. I shouldn't have to tell you that when you have the text in front of you!" My heart plummeted through the manhole cover and tears rose through my throat.

"I understand. I'll let you go. Thanks for your time."

"I'm sorry to be harsh," Romy said more gently. "I

know it's not you demanding an answer. Please understand, this is my career, my reputation, at stake."

"Yes, of course. I'm sorry!" I slammed down the phone and ran for the handicapped bathroom. On the cold, white tile, I curled into the smallest ball I could manage for my oversized body and rocked until my sobbing subsided.

WHEN I CREPT BACK to my desk, a calendar notification was sounding. I'd forgotten my appointment with Dr. Drexler. I called right away.

"Vi, this is Michelle Black. I'm sorry, I can't be there this afternoon. I'm swamped at work."

"Do you want next Monday or Wednesday? She's on vacation for three weeks after that."

"Wednesday," I set a reminder. "Oh! Vi?" I called, hoping she was still there.

"Yes?"

"The ER doctor prescribed Xanax for me, but I don't want to run out. Could you please ask Dr. Drexler to refill it before I come in?"

"Sure, I'll have her send it to the pharmacy."

When I hung up, the message light on my phone began blinking. It hadn't rung while I talked to Vi, so whoever it was placed the call through the trunk and selected my voicemail rather than risk me answering. I played the message.

"Michelle, this is Romy. I thought about our conversation. I can't sit on this. I'm taking the information to my manager, Richard. After he and I

talk, I'll get back to you about what steps we're taking."
I sprinted to Monica's office, seeking cover and assistance. It was empty and dark. Staring into the bouncing geometric figures of her screensaver, I lost all sense of time and place. Josh discovered me there.

"Michelle, long time, no see. Are you looking for Monica?" My eyes, wide and staring, took in his face.

"Josh, I'm not sure what to do. I think I gave information to Westing that may cause them to downgrade us!"

"Was it accidental?"

"No, Jay told me to preview the acquisition with Romy. I told him it wasn't a good idea, but he insisted. Now she's gone to her boss and is considering what actions to take."

"She doesn't like the acquisition?"

"No, she doesn't! It says clearly in her last note that this kind of strategic departure would be viewed negatively. I don't understand why Jay told me to do this!"

"Then why did you do it?" It was too absurd to say *because I'm scared of Jay*.

"I don't know."

"I don't envy you. You're going to have to tell Jay what happened, but don't let it be a surprise to Monica or Edith. Better tell them first." The can of worms got bigger. I was going to have to admit what happened to my whole management chain! "I think they're all in the same meeting. Maybe Penny can help you get a hold of them."

I raced to the executive floor, where I found Penny's

desk deserted and all the doors yawning on empty offices. I overheard Jay say goodbye in a conference room. Edith's and Monica's voices bid adieu. I rushed in, but Jay had already hit end.

"Jay! I need to talk to you and Edith and Monica!" He leaned back in his cushy leather chair at the head of the conference room table.

"They've gone into another meeting."

"There's a problem with The Westing Group."

"Take a seat after you close the door," no ripple disturbed his calm demeanor. "Monica and Edith don't need to be bothered with this. What's the problem?" I relayed my conversation with Romy.

"...then, she left a voicemail saying that she's going to her manager. I'm waiting to hear back."

"This isn't a new strategic direction," Jay complained. "It's a relatively small acquisition!"

"Romy sees it as another step down the path away from our strengths."

"She's wrong, and it's *your job* to make her see that."

"Jay, she made her opinion crystal clear. She's already talking to Richard!"

"Then, we need to get our point-of-view in front of him so he can help us redirect her." A simple truth had been lost in all this maneuvering: the acquisition forecast didn't look good for us. I swallowed my fear and spoke my mind.

"What about the fact that our forecast doesn't support the acquisition? The numbers don't pencil in any version I've seen. The profit erosion is enough to justify a downgrade, as I've said before."

"You don't need to worry about that. The Financial Planning team is massaging the forecast. You need to worry about keeping Romy from downgrading us until we have the right numbers to show her." My body went cold.

"What happens when she sees the next public filings after we complete the acquisition and the numbers look different?"

"Acquisitions never go the way they're expected to on paper. It's your job to help her see beyond the numbers, into the story. Go make the story sizzle."

As had happened so often lately, I found myself triggered, transported into the midst of another memory. This one was dredged up from shortly after the Wisconsin debacle.

DAMIEN, who was my manager before Monica, faced me across the vast expanse of an oak desk. Newly promoted, I brimmed with confidence and edgy ideas. I slid a half-inch thick stack of paper over to him.

"Here's my recommendation. We can improve the existing process and drive a whole point, maybe two, of savings in the first quarter!" Damien's reaction was indecipherable as he flipped through pages.

"The process you're proposing to change has always been done the way it is now."

"Yes, but new regulations allow us to change. The industry will inevitably go this way. We can be on the leading edge."

"We aren't aspiring to be industry leaders," he said as he leaned away from me but kept his fingertips tented over the stack of paper. "This proposal is too forward-thinking for our management team." To give him an easy yes, I made an offer.

"If it would help, I'd be happy to present the idea straight to Jay to save you the time and effort." He picked up the presentation, pinching it between index finger and thumb.

"Why would you threaten to go over my head?" he narrowed his eyes, and I had the fleeting thought that he was about to throw the ceramic mug he held in his other hand. Instead, he curled his lip and flung the presentation across the desk between us. The pages flew apart, a flock of white doves coming at my face. I froze in shock. Paper fluttered to the floor. "Take that and get out."

I crawled under his desk and around the chair I'd occupied to collect my rejected work. He stared out the window, sipping coffee, till I left.

THE MEMORY WOUND DOWN. Jay waited expectantly. I couldn't argue with him, but I couldn't agree, either.

"I don't know how to do that," I whispered.

"What do you mean, you don't know how?" I stared at him, deadening my body. He made an impatient sound. "Fine, arrange a time to call Richard. I'll take care of it myself."

I fled, hiding out in the bathroom until enough time

passed that I expected my call to Romy's boss in New York would reach an empty office. A wave of nausea hit when his assistant answered, and I was struck mute.

"Hello? Is anyone there?"

"Yes, I'm sorry. This is Michelle Black. Is Richard around this week?"

"You're in luck, Michelle! He's still here. Let me transfer you," she was gone, and Richard was on the line before I could plunge the handset into the cradle.

"Hi, Michelle. How can I help you?"

"Hi, Richard," my voice was as thready as my pulse. "Jay asked me to schedule a call with you tomorrow..."

I spent the remainder of the day in half-hour shifts, alternately trying to work at my desk and snuffing out panic attacks in the bathroom.

LIKE GROUNDHOG DAY, I ended up in the same place the next morning. Desperate for any excuse to cancel the upcoming call with Jay and Richard, I played Russian roulette with my contacts around the company. My first call was to a senior vice president in Financial Planning.

"Hi, Gwen. How are the numbers looking?" If the projected acquisition results were better than Romy expected, I hoped she wouldn't be able to justify a downgrade.

"Sorry, I can't answer that yet. Jay's got us running a ton of scenarios with wide variations." Next, I tried our Communications department.

"Aaron! I'm glad I caught you."

"I'm dodging press inquiries about the rumored acquisition. What's up?"

"I was hoping you could tell me what the CEO thinks of this transaction." If our CEO knew the headwinds we faced, I hoped he would pull the plug.

"Sorry, Michelle. Stan's on all internal meetings. I'm on outbound communications only right now." Stan, our Chief Communications Officer, was an infamous information hog. I didn't even bother contacting him. I chewed on my fingers and sucked blood from the open wounds, fantasizing about warm Hawaiian sun and turquoise water while debating my next move. I considered calling our Chief Corporate Counsel, but I was terrified of Jay discovering my borderline insubordination.

The phone rang.

Without looking, I knew it was Romy. I knew why she was calling. I could feel her ire in my empath sense. I let voicemail pick up and stared at the phone, silently begging the message light to start blinking. I jumped when it rang again. The last thing I wanted was for her to hang up and try Jay's office. Heart pounding, I answered.

"This is Michelle."

"Michelle, this is Romy at Westing. We need to talk. My boss, Richard, surprised me this morning when he asked the subject of our upcoming call. I don't have a call scheduled with you. That leads me to assume one thing; that you went to him in an attempt to circumnavigate me. I'm aware that your management team is unhappy with my opinion, but I never expected this."

"Romy, I'm sorry. Jay told me to—" she stopped me.

"Let me be clear. I am not comfortable with what you're asking me to do. Please deliver the message to Jay that The Westing Group will react appropriately to *public* announcements. There is no need for a call this afternoon because there is nothing to discuss until the deal is public!"

"Please, Romy! Can you and Richard take the call?" I begged. "Maybe if Jay hears directly from you, it will make a difference." Romy sighed. I felt her soften, but her voice was still brittle.

"Fine, but beware. If I feel like your management is trying to ramrod us ever again, I will not hesitate to write about their actions and downgrade your rating. Talk to you this afternoon." The phone went dead. I almost fell out of my chair when it rang again. Nearly an hour had gone by as I stared into space, listening to the off-kilter beating of my heart. It was Penny, Jay's assistant.

"Jay wants to know what time the Westing call is."

"Eleven."

"With Richard, right? What's his title?"

"Senior vice president. Oh, and—" I bit my lips.

"Yes?"

"Nothing." I'd been on the verge of telling her to add Romy to the invite.

"Thanks. Jay will step out of the staff meeting to take the call in his office. He wants you to come up."

Nervously I watched the clock. I tried wading

through the morass of emails in my inbox, but their emergency tone was tinder to the dry brush of my anxiety. Instead of retreating to the bathroom as had become my habit, I clicked open a web browser in one monitor and a blank document in the other, inserting earbuds for camouflage.

AT A QUARTER TO ELEVEN, I surveyed my work. The schedule for our Hawaii trip was taking shape. There was a list of a dozen Oahu beaches needing further research, four luaus to call about, and three ideas for day trips. Still, I felt no corresponding sense of accomplishment. The impending vacation was beginning to feel less like a safe harbor and more like a forced march.

As if to drive the point home, my inbox had topped up with two dozen more emails. I couldn't read them. I wouldn't. I highlighted the clamoring messages and moused over the garbage can.

I unhighlighted them.

I put my monitor to sleep and gathered what I needed for the Westing call. I pressed my lips together, woke my monitor, re-highlighted the offending missives, and hit delete.

Upstairs, Jay's office door was closed.

"He's on the line," Penny said. "He wants you to go in."

"Why is he on already?"

"I forwarded you an email. He ended his staff meeting early." Fuming at myself for deleting things unread, I pushed into Jay's office. Richard was on speaker.

"...Romy came to me about a rumored acquisition. Off the record, we're not comfortable with it as an opportunity for your company."

Romy jumped in with, "In fact, were you to pursue it, it would validate the concerns I laid out in my most recent note." I felt Jay's shock at hearing her voice. He jabbed the mute button.

"Why is Romy on this call?" he demanded. I shrugged helplessly and lied.

"Richard must have told her about it." He unmuted the call and forced a jovial tone.

"Well, hello, Romy! I didn't know you were going to be on with us."

"Gee, I don't know why not. Michelle invited me," Romy replied waspishly. Jay shot me a glare that made my insides wither. I locked every muscle against my flight response.

"Michelle just joined us. I guess she didn't have time to warn me."

"I wouldn't think you'd need a warning that your primary analyst would be on a call about such an important topic," Romy chided.

Jay tried to laugh off his discomfort with a wry, "Touché."

"While I appreciate Richard's willingness to share our unofficial thoughts with you," Romy continued, "let us set the record straight. The Westing Group no longer entertains previews of acquisitions. We are not able to give informal opinions. Michelle has a copy of the ethics code that explains the embargo, which she told me she shared with you."

"Yes, Michelle has done that," Jay kept his eyes down.

"Good. You also have the note I wrote a few months ago. My opinion was unambiguous. We will not take any more calls like this. We can only react to public announcements, just like the rest of the Street."

"We know it's a tough transition," Richard smoothed over Romy's unsympathetic delivery. "You're not the only ones confused by the new rules and process."

"I understand," Jay said. "Thanks for taking the time. Michelle will be in touch if we go ahead with the acquisition," he ended the call. I was rooted to the spot where I'd stopped when I walked in. He kept his eyes down. I forced myself to speak while fighting the overwhelming urge to flee.

"I have a new version of my analysis. Do you want to see it? I think we might be able to convince Romy that her view is pessimistic."

"We are done here."

"Do you want me to—"

"I said we are done. Shut the door when you leave."

CHAPTER 11

*J*ay and I had no further one-on-one contact after the uncomfortable call with Westing. While my desk had gone silent, others had not. My final contribution would come at the very end, when forecasting was complete and ready to present to our CEO and Board of Directors.

Meanwhile, I set my obsessive anxiety to work on vacation plans. Over dinner each night, I recited my research findings for Ed in painstaking detail. He listened patiently; then, we repeated a similar conversation on the subject *du jour*.

"…that's why I think we should choose between these two beaches for Wednesday morning. Or at least prioritize them. If we don't like the first one, we can move on to the runner up. The main thing is, I don't want us to be stuck somewhere we're miserable without a backup plan. But these beaches are both on one side of the island. What if we decide we don't want to be on that side? What do you think?"

"Sounds good, Shell," his easy acceptance was making me crazy.

"Which one do you think is better?" I pressured.

"I'm sure you picked the two perfect beaches for that day," he assured me. I wanted more than this tacit agreement. Anxiety had become my Pavlovian response to every uncertainty, even tiny ones. I *needed* to know what we were going to be doing that day on Oahu. Even more, I *needed* his shared ownership because I no longer trusted myself to make decisions. Our discussion always ended with me yelling.

"Fine! I'll decide, and you better not complain even once!" Then I'd mark up all the potential combinations of choosing one beach, or both, in either order, on the vacation schedule that was beginning to look like a Gantt chart from hell.

Terrified of forgetting something, I resorted to making lists for the trip. List-making was the only activity that made me feel grounded. There was a list of my clothes to take, another for Ed's clothes, another for kids' clothes. Each of us had a toiletries list and a medications list. Then there were the swimwear and gear lists. I made lists of documents I thought we needed to carry. My list of lists was endless. Each day, I reviewed my lists many times. If I got off-track while examining them, I started over again from the beginning. Sometimes, when my anxiety crested, I wrote and rewrote them longhand, filling my trash can with basketballs of crumpled paper.

· · ·

THE DAY before the big meeting, I called luau companies from my desk at work. I referred to my list of luau questions, asking exhaustive minutiae about which dishes they offered, what the entertainment was like, how much leis cost, where to find parking at what price. I was relieved when a call from Troy interrupted my repetitive ticking down the list.

"Did you hear?" he asked.

"No, what?"

"We're going to pass on the acquisition. It turns out the target is a real stinker. They're covering up major profitability problems."

"Who told you?"

"Gwen," he referred to our colleague in Financial Planning. I added her to the call.

"Is it true we're going to pass?" I asked. She was slow to reply.

"I thought for sure when my boss went to Jay with the forecast it was dead in the water! The numbers don't make sense. But when Abhay returned, he shook his head at me and closed himself in his office. I'm waiting to find out what happened."

"Thanks, can you let me or Troy know?"

"Will do," she hung up. Troy stayed on the line and asked me a question.

"If we know the rating agencies are biased against this deal and the numbers don't look great, why would we even think of going through with it?" I couldn't think of a single reason why.

. . .

LATE THAT AFTERNOON, I fought to stay awake through the stupor of too much Xanax. Dr. Drexler had come through with a 60-pill supply, causing me to abandon all restraint. Without the synergy of the painkillers, however, what little high I could achieve was disappointing. My phone rang, and Jay barked through my headset.

"Get the version of the forecast Gwen's working on now. Run the rating agency analysis and send me everything before you leave," he hung up without waiting for my assent. I reminded myself, *"I just have to make it to Hawaii."*

I called Gwen to relay Jay's directive.

"Abhay's reviewing the final forecast," she told me. "I'll send it to you as soon as he says okay." My empath sense registered her perturbation.

"It doesn't sound like we're abandoning ship," I probed.

"Nope."

"I take it you're not thrilled?"

"This isn't a good company to buy!" she erupted. "Others would do the same thing for us and are a better fit—" she stopped, then finished resignedly. "The decision is above my pay grade. All I can do is follow orders at this point." When she sent me the forecast, the numbers were far more compelling than earlier iterations. I wanted to call back and ask why, but I didn't. I took another Xanax and kept working.

IT WAS after ten p.m. when I arrived home. Still, Jay

called as I was getting ready for bed, setting my teeth on edge.

"Tomorrow before the meeting, get me a ten-year history of our target's credit rating and correlate it with profitability. Don't call any of the rating agencies or anyone internally. Deliver it directly to me." This was not an insignificant request. I wanted to ask why he needed it, but I didn't. I tossed and turned, wondering what wild goose chase he'd sent me on.

At 4:30 a.m., I boarded the first BART train of the day, strung out and afraid to take the amount of Xanax that would wipe out the worry whirring in my guts. In my office on the deserted fifteenth floor, I fired up my Bloomberg. All morning I worked on Jay's request. He called two hours before the big meeting.

"Bring me what you have."

"The history is incomplete," I informed him.

"I don't care. I need whatever you have now." He hung up. My empath sense was zinging, but Gwen's words from the day before rang in my head. This was above my pay grade.

AT THE APPOINTED TIME, Monica and I headed up to the virtual conference room, where we would connect with our CEO and Board of Directors via a real-time satellite link. A host of our most senior colleagues chatted in subdued tones in the anteroom. One of them broke away when we arrived. It was Stan, the Chief Communications Officer whom I had chosen not to call in my game of Russian roulette.

"Michelle, may I have a moment?" he waylaid me as Monica continued into the conference room. "The Gazette called yesterday with questions about this rumored acquisition. It seems the reporter has a source at The Westing Group. His source told him that, if we complete this transaction, we will be downgraded because the target's rating is so low." I wanted to ask why he hadn't called me as soon as he hung up from talking to the reporter, but Jay's warning not to discuss the target's rating echoed in my head. I tried to give enough of an answer in a sufficiently surly tone to make Stan go away.

"Jay and I previewed the acquisition with our team at Westing. I'm sure they're on top of things." He waited expectantly, but I was afraid to say more.

"I see. Thank you," Stan bowed his head to me and retreated to his clique. Concerned, I sought out Monica, who was already seated in her conference room chair.

"Stan just told me he received a tip from a reporter at The Gazette!" I repeated the rest of Stan's revelation in a hushed whisper, then added, "I think Romy put in a call to them." Monica twisted in her seat to look at me.

"Why would Romy have done that? She doesn't know about this acquisition yet." Too late, I realized my mistake. I'd neglected to share with my boss the fact or substance of Jay's and my call to Romy and Richard. My heart skipped. What if Jay had meant I was *never* supposed to tell Monica or Edith about our conversation with Westing? What if Romy mentioned it to them, though? Standing there open-mouthed, I second- and third-guessed what to do.

"Jay and I talked to her," I finally confessed. Monica's eyes widened. I rushed to add, "Only in broad terms! And Romy's boss, Richard, was on the phone, too." Her eyes went from wide to incredulous.

"*Romy* allowed this under the new rules?"

"Yes, but she said they wouldn't do it again," I felt Monica's surprise morph into anger.

"Michelle, you know the new rules Westing put in place. I'm shocked that you allowed Jay to make such a call," her displeasure pummeled me like water sprayed from a fire hydrant. "It's *your job* to keep him out of the trouble that could come from accidental leaks before we announce publicly!"

Just then, Jay walked in.

"I'm going to let Jay know what Stan said," I squeaked before I rushed over and appealed to him. "May I please speak with you in the small conference room?"

"It's time to begin the meeting," he said, avoiding my eyes. I willed him to feel my urgency, fighting to keep my voice calm.

"This is important. It's about our Westing Group rating." I felt his shiver of concern. He followed me to the other room where I faced him and parroted Stan's disclosure.

Jay didn't say anything. I started to wonder if he'd heard me because neither his expression nor his energy changed. My empath sense was stymied. This situation seemed like a big deal, but all of my confidence in my own discernment had eroded. Maybe I was wrong.

"Who did Stan tell other than you?" Jay finally asked.

"I don't know. It was just Stan and me in the anteroom." Jay folded his arms.

"Our business decisions should not be driven by fear of a rating downgrade. This acquisition is a good opportunity. Everyone, including Romy, will see that when it's done!" He swung open the door and strode out. I realized I'd been holding my breath and I was poised on tiptoes, ready to run away, but I didn't know where I'd go. My feet got as far as the bathroom. I splashed cold water on my face, then curled my upper lip at my reflection in the mirror.

"Get your ass in that conference room!" I hissed. "You warned Jay. The rest is above your pay grade." With a rough paper towel, I swiped away sink water and tears.

WHEN I RETURNED to the big videoconference room, Jay was still absent. Too nervous to sit, I handed out copies of my presentation.

"Hello again, Michelle," greeted Mason, the Chief Marketing Officer. "You seem more collected than when we met at the elevator! How're things going?"

"The Westing Group is not happy," I grimaced, "but I can't do anything about it!"

"When are the credit rating agencies happy about anything?" Mason laughed. "It's their job to believe the sky is falling!" I hoped he was right. I hoped Jay was right and that all the negative expectations of this acquisition would prove unfounded. I hoped *someone* was right because I was never right anymore.

Jay finally reappeared and found his seat beside Mason, in front of Monica and me. Mason swiveled around and crooked his finger at me. I leaned across the table that separated us.

"Can I please get another copy of your deck?" he whispered. "Mine seems to have something smudged on it." Mortified, I recognized the streaky marks to which he was pointing. My shredded fingers had left bloody brown-red smudges on the paper. Mason's whisper drew Jay's attention. Jay swiveled around, too, but he didn't whisper.

"Disgusting. It looks like someone wiped the bathroom floor with it!" I pressed my lips together and passed an extra copy to Mason, careful to complete the transaction using only the pads of fingers that weren't weeping or bleeding. Monica covertly studied my hands. I drew them inside my suit jacket and tried to wipe away congealed blood while Jay called the meeting to order. My heart was hammering, and every inch of me tingled. I wished I would have a heart attack right then; all else be damned. I wanted to die.

FOR THE BETTER PART OF two hours, Jay extolled the virtues of our acquisition target to the CEO and Board of Directors. A moderate, unsurprising Q&A session followed. Then, he focused on the screen image of the CEO, for whom we were performing this dog-and-pony show.

"I recommend we proceed with this acquisition," he finished.

The CEO leaned back in his chair, fingers tented under his chin. Tension stretched like giant suspension bridge cables through the satellite feed, connecting everyone who awaited his verdict.

"You do not expect a rating downgrade when we announce this acquisition," he offered the observation for Jay to confirm or deny.

"We do not. Our ratings are solid, except for the negative outlook from The Westing Group. We previewed the acquisition with them. I'm confident that any doubts they harbor will be settled upon successful completion."

"My first concern is that we retain our strength, and our position as one of the largest players in the industry. It would be disastrous for us to be downgraded as a result of a small acquisition such as this."

"A downgrade wouldn't make sense," Jay minimized the concern. "Westing would be the laughingstock of Wall Street if they did."

"Your assessment doesn't agree with what Stan told me," the CEO frowned. I didn't have to see Jay's face to know it paled. I held my breath, along with everyone else in the meeting.

"What did Stan tell you?" Jay asked. I couldn't believe my ears. Had he forgotten my panicked entreaty to him before the start of this meeting? The CEO peered through the camera to find Stan, seated four places down from me. Stan cleared his throat.

"Jay, as I informed Michelle Black in advance of this

meeting, Westing is poised to downgrade us if this acquisition is approved."

In nightmarish slow-motion, Jay turned to me.

"Michelle, is this true?" he feigned astonishment. I was speechless, tongue cleaved to the roof of my mouth. I looked at Monica. She wore an expectant expression. I looked at Stan. He sat at attention, staring into the screen at the front of the room. Motes of color danced behind my eyes, and I wondered if a stroke could be causing them.

"I don't know," I whispered.

"What do you mean, *you don't know*?" Jay prompted. There was no way for me to answer without calling him a liar to his face, in front of the CEO. Panic engulfed me.

"I don't know any other contacts at Westing!" I almost shrieked the nonsense excuse. Edith, who was always suave in a pinch, jumped in to save me.

"Jay, I think what Michelle is saying is, we've concentrated our efforts solely on defending our company's rating. Given Westing's unexpected focus on this target, it seems appropriate to begin analyzing the ratings of all of our targets. Does that sound like the right way to proceed?" Edith's question hung in the air. Jay kept staring at me, his back to the screen where everyone waited. If I opened my mouth, I would vomit. I kept it closed. He broke eye contact and swiveled to face forward.

"Obviously, in light of Stan's news, we cannot recommend moving forward with this acquisition." I felt his acute embarrassment, whitewashed with an imperious tone. Then, he threw me under the bus. "It's clear that our rating agency relationships have been sorely neglected. Expect to hear from my office in the fall with a new strategic plan for rating agency relations."

The CEO untented his fingers and sat forward, nodding.

"This is the best course of action," he agreed with Jay. "Let's put the acquisition program on hiatus while we strengthen our relationships with the rating agencies, so we're not surprised again. This meeting is adjourned!"

The words released me from the agonizing thrall that held me frozen in place, and I shot out the door like a rocket.

CHAPTER 12

July 2015

*A*fter parting ways in the Red Robin parking lot, we exchanged naughty pics and sexts every couple of days. There was an aloofness, true to our infidelitous pact, in the asynchronous conversation we shared. Unlike with the other men I explored, it didn't bother me when a days-long silence stretched between us. Somehow, I knew you'd always be there when I texted next. We were both seeking something, and we tacitly accepted each other's search.

A window of opportunity to consummate our affair opened on a weekday morning in July. Like all the cheating women I witnessed in all the movies about cheating I ever saw, I squished into a fancy matching lingerie set. I remembered your favorite color. My undies were hot pink, purchased specially for today. I bought a lot of inaugural panty sets around that time. I kept them like trophies under my bed, folded carefully into a giant plastic storage box with wheels.

When you arrived, you texted.

"You here?"

"Yes," I tapped back, waiting by the front door. We'd agreed in advance that you would park down the block. A couple of minutes passed. My stomach twisted when I heard you step onto the front porch. I swung open the door, and your eyes punched me in the gut. The lightning strike at IKEA flashed upon me. I'd forgotten it in the weeks since it happened.

"Hi," you said as you entered the home I shared with my husband and kids and debt and depression. And two dogs. It dawned on me that the dogs were oddly calm. They sniffed at you curiously and wiggle-danced before they ignored us.

"Those are awesome guard dogs," you observed. We laughed, nerves easing. Our attention turned to each other. You advanced into my space, leaning down to kiss me. Around us, I could feel the cone-shaped halo of light that I'd seen so clearly at Red Robin. Your arms around my waist and my arms around your neck created a time warp like a lasso encircling us as the clock downshifted. You were velvet against my face, warm tongue reaching into my mouth. I forgot to exhale or inhale.

With a backward step, I broke contact. Comically, you stayed poised for a second in a bent-down shape, duck lips left hanging. I beckoned you to follow me. Your eyes settled on my soft black robe when we entered the master bedroom and faced each other.

Insecurity gripped me. I breathed deep and reminded myself what these trysts brought with them. My fix had arrived. Loneliness would be held at bay for an hour or two. Perhaps I would begin to feel human again, like I deserved to be alive, by the end. I pushed aside fear and stepped close to you. We tangled together.

My body responded to yours involuntarily, sweat slicking the small of my back as my heart leaped to a gallop. Wetness rushed in hot pink panties, arriving with the same sharp pang of desire I'd felt for you last time we met. We ended up naked on the bed before I could even wrap my mind around the fact that I liked kissing you. Kissing was always a chore before you.

We spent an hour exploring and experimenting with what our bodies could do together. Every position we found, every movement we made, our bodies knew each other. Yours fit me in a way no other had ever melded to mine. A familiar wave built between us. I came hard as you moved inside of me. The sweeping release caught me off guard. We lay beside each other to catch our breath.

"That was intense," your voice was solemn.

"Yes, it was," I confirmed. There were no other words. It took longer than usual for the fog of shame and self-loathing to overflow its dam inside me. You dressed after a few minutes. I rewrapped the soft black robe, following you to the door. You turned to me, and I could see that you held in place a mask over your face. I wanted to rip it off after the intimacy of the past hour, but my own restrictive costume was already firmly reaffixed.

"Thank you," you said stiffly. I laughed, thinking how strange it was that you thanked me for cheating on our spouses together. With a peck on the lips and a terse, "I'll text you later," you were gone.

To be continued...

Made in the USA
Monee, IL
19 July 2020